LIKE SECOND SKIN

TARA MOELLER

DreamPunk Press

Copyright © 2025 by Tara Moeller

All rights reserved.

978-1-963928-02-0 Garamond
978-1-963928-03-7 Open Dyslexic
978-1-963928-04-4 ePub

No portion of this book may be reproduced in any form without written permission from the publisher or author, except as permitted by U.S. copyright law.

Prologue

28 Nov 2114

F ROM: Consolidated Forces of the Republic Recruiting Center, Columbia District

TO: Kaalinda Vesta MacReady

Citizen MacReady,

This serves as your notification that you are drafted to the CFoR as of your eighteenth birthday on 6 December 2114. You are directed to report to the CFoR Recruiting Center, Columbia District, for transport to the recruit processing depot and initial measure of suitability testing. Please bring a copy of your birth certificate, your official travel pass, and any corroborating medical claims, signed by three CFoR-certified medical practitioners if you plan to protest this draft.

If initial measure testing shows you are not fit for military duty, you will be transferred to the Humanitarian Service Corps of the Republic, where you will serve for 2 years in patriotic support of civilian citizen projects or overseas humanitarian missions.

Upon release from 2 years of such service or 4years military service, you will receive an outgoing benefits package equal to one year of pay at the minimum wage on that date or two years tuition-free at a CFoR-sponsored technical school. The CFoR will determine the benefit package for which you qualify. If your service is deemed exemplary, you may be offered the opportunity to re-enlist in either the CFoR or the HSCoR, as determined by the CFoR.

If you do not survive your service, whether in the CFoR or the HSCoR, such benefit package may, at a reduced rate, be offered to your nearest kin as identified in your enlistment paperwork. This benefit package may be offered in addition to any benefit package the identified nearest kin has earned of their own merit by service (as determined by the CFoR).

The CFoR looks forward to processing you on 6December 2114. It is suggested that you arrive at least one hour before your scheduled arrival time to ensure you are not logged as a no-show.

E. B. Smith, Jr
Acting Proletariat-General of the CFoR/Director Supreme of the HSCoR

∞ Determine to be the RIGHT in the WORLD ∞

1

Chapter 1

7 Dec 2114

Kaalinda was almost at the front of the line. She'd been standing, waiting, most of the morning. A morning that had started with an abrupt wake-up blast at 0400.

The recruit in front of her surged forward, almost tripping in his haste to keep up with the soldier that grabbed him; he was strapped down into the large metal chair that held center stage at the front of the room.

She thought he had introduced himself as Balderas. Remembering bits of their hushed, rambling conversation since queuing up, Kaalinda knew he had a large family out West, and that he had nearly completed technical school exams before getting his draft letter.

That put him at least a couple of years ahead of her.

Technicians in starched dull green jackets stuck test probes to the temples of Balderas' newly shaven head, only short fuzzy spikes of damp blond hair remaining on the very top. Sweat beaded along his pale brow, his hands clenched the arms of the chair. Dark half-moons outlined the bright blue of his eyes, making the whites appear supernaturally white.

Kaalinda ran her shaky right hand over her own head, feeling the soft fuzz left by the shears. It felt odd. Until early that morning, her long auburn hair had never been cut above her shoulders. She had been told that it was her best feature, that the thick red curls were the perfect frame for her heart-shaped face. Sparing a vain moment, she wondered what it looked like now, but had trouble imagining it.

She glanced down at her nails. Yesterday, they had been long, manicured, with a shiny apple-red polish. But harsh chemicals had been used to take off the paint, turning them a yellowy-orange, then cut almost to the nail bed. Straight across, the corners jagged and sharp, miniature talons that scratched her skin.

Shifting her weight, Kaalinda pulled up on her pants. The light blue cotton pajama-like outfit she had been given last night hung on her slight frame, emphasizing her slender neck. The cuffs of the pants were rolled twice so she wouldn't stumble, and the fabric belt of the top was wrapped twice around her narrow waist.

A soft noise from Balderas caught her attention, drawing her thoughts back to the room and what was happening around her.

Balderas sat quiet, eyes blinking and twitching, watching the scientists work at the controls of the machine. The large room buzzed with activity, making the long, silent, unmoving line of potential soldiers seem out of place; a power cord attached to a glittering Rube Goldberg contraption.

Kaalinda craned her head to watch the would-be soldiers behind her. She couldn't remember all their names, but she recognized some of their faces. They all shared a similar expression: awe mixed with trepidation.

The recruits stood in a crooked line, staring at the machine, the scientists, and the room around them. They kept their eyes from settling on Balderas.

Kaalinda could smell old sweat, and, if she wasn't mistaken, the stronger smell of urine. Looking down at the floor, she could see older stains, as well as more recent additions in the form of small, yellow puddles.

She tightened the muscles of her pelvis and returned her thoughts to her purpose. She needed to pass the machine's test.

Kill. Kill. Kill. Kaalinda repeated the litany to herself and turned back to face the scientists.

The machine attached to the probes hummed, starting low before increasing pitch to a shrieking whine. Lights flickered across a large grey screen, the pixels of wavy red lines undulating. The technicians watched the screen, the lights and waves reflecting on their eyeglass lenses, each making notes on a small electronic notepad.

Kaalinda's nerves stretched tighter, her stomach burned. She took a deep breath, releasing it slowly, rationing the air through her nostrils, huffing it out until there was nothing of it left in her lungs before slowly, carefully sucking air back in. The burning liquid began to recede.

Kill.

She concentrated on the single word, barely registering the movements of the scientists or Balderas, still attached to the machine.

Oh, God, the machine.

The panic she'd felt at her first sight of it returned. The short briefing that morning had not prepared her for the towering array of lights, buttons, and dials that took up an entire wall of the room. The square gray screen, with those tiny waves traveling across it from right to left, was as tall as a man. A twisted mix of multicolored wires connected the machine to the metal chair. The chair sat on a wide rubber platform. It had special pads for the recruit's feet, and thin, cotton-web straps held legs and arms in place.

The technicians, dressed in green scrubs and white lab coats, darted around the room, dodging each other's movements like it was a familiar choreographed dance. Their hair was cropped short, though longer than the hair of the recruits. Those with glasses wore the thin, wire-rimmed type that were standard military issue. Rubber-soled shoes kept their movements silent on the tile floor, only the occasional misstep in urine lending a sound.

Kaalinda could only tell them apart by the color of the nametags they wore.

The machine ceased its annoying whine, leaving a blank silence. The technicians gathered in a small circle in front of the screen, notepads out, whispering among themselves.

One shook his head. At this signal, two armed soldiers, standing near a pair of doors at one end of the room, marched forward; his red badge must mean he was in charge.

The guards grabbed Balderas, ripped the probes off, and dragged him through the doors. One technician stepped forward with a yellow, stained towel and wiped off the chair. His movements drew Kaalinda's gaze, and she noticed the pale amber puddle on the floor in front of the chair.

The technician with the red badge motioned Kaalinda forward. "Ready?" He spoke more to the electronic tablet in his hands than to Kaalinda, his fingers flying over the touch screen. Without waiting for her to answer, he motioned for her to take the chair.

Kaalinda did as she was bid, trying to settle herself in the large, uncomfortable chair.

Kill. Kill. Kill. She kept the litany repeating in her head.

That was what they wanted right; someone willing to kill?

Placing her bare feet and hands on the pads, Kaalinda felt the remnants of warmth left by Balderas and all the recruits tested before him. Curling her hands into the grooves, she watched one technician—his eyes almost covered by eyebrows longer than the hair on the top of his head—wrap the straps around her wrists then bend to place the straps around her feet. The gel used to attach the probes was cold and sticky: an icy shock against the hot skin of her face. A dull ache began in her temples.

Kaalinda tried to listen to the bushy-browed technician repeat the whispered monologue that was the explanation of what was about to happen.

"...discomfort, but the low-frequency waves will do no real damage to your body tissue. The probes are both transmitter and receiver, introducing the signal to your body, then, relaying the returned signal along the wires back to the machine, where they will be interpreted. The machine will note any differences between the waves exiting your body and the original: Things like distortion, amplitude, and signal strength. From the results, we will make out determination."

Kaalinda stared straight ahead. The smell of nervous sweat from the recruits mixed with the too-sweet smell of burnt starch from the technicians' lab coats made her stomach roil.

She concentrated on keeping her fear from showing on her face, on maintaining her focus. Her fingers grasped the arms of the chair so hard the blood vessels on the backs of her hands bulged from the pressure. Shifting in the seat, she tried to dislodge the damp cotton shirtthat stuck to her armpits and back. Its coolness caused tiny goose bumps to appear on her arms, the pale body hair standing up, like the fur on the back ofa hissing cat.

The technicians retreated to their stations at the controls. Kaalinda tuned them out, concentrating solely on one word: KILL. She licked pale, anxious lips, trying to wet them with a dry tongue. Instead, she caught the salty remnants of sweat on her upper lip, wincing at its sting.

Oh, God, what I wouldn't do for a glass of water right now.

The machine hummed; the chair vibrated. The test began.

Kaalinda's palms and the bottoms of her feet grew warm. A sensation like hundreds of tiny needles pricking her, started at her lower back, and slowly crept upwards. She couldn't stop the instinctive stiffening of her muscles, the slight arching of her back.

The hum was inside of her, intensifying to a dull throb, her blood pumping to the same, rapid rhythm.

It became a whine, rattling in her eardrums, pain shooting through to her brain.

A low chatter started among the technicians, the noise rising above the constant whine of the machine. They stared at the screen. Lights blinked faster. They all nodded as one.

The sound of the machine changed pitch, first getting deeper, then getting higher. The waves on the screen grew larger as one technician, his blue nametag drooping at one end, increased magnification.

Kaalinda started in the chair when the machine stopped. The loss of noise was so intense it was as if something had been physically removed from the room.

The pain was gone, too, just as sudden, leaving a numbness that was unsettling. It was like something tangible had left her body.

The line of recruits shifted, almost as one body, rather than many. Their eyes darted from Kaalinda, still strapped in the chair, to the technicians, busily entering data into their notepads.

The one in charge—his red badge still the only one in that color she could see—marched toward Kaalinda, stopping in front of her. He removed the probes and straps, then handed her a small tablet. A wide grin split a face that had been otherwise austere.

Kaalinda thought he might be pleased.

"Check that all the information is correct." He then stood silent, waiting, hands folded in front of his thin brushed-metal belt buckle.

She looked over the small square card.
    NAME –Kaalinda Vesta MacReady
    AGE   - 18 DOB – 06 December 2096
    HEIGHT –1.7m   WEIGHT – 52kg
"It's correct."

"Sign and date on the bottom line then press your thumb to the square next to it." He handed her a standard stylus.

She signed her name, slow, her muscles lagging the direction from her brain, the usual even loops a little shaky and misshaped, faltering a bit on the date format, settling for day-month-year: 07 Dec 2114.She pressed her thumb to the square and it flashed green before displaying a black depiction of her thumbprint.

"Congratulations, you are now an enlisted member of the Consolidated Forces of the Republic."

Kaalinda sighed in relief, a slight smile playing around her lips; twin spots of pink blooming in her cheeks.

"Excited?" He asked, his dark eyes staring, narrowing just a bit. He was close enough now for Kaalinda to read the red nametag: Smythe.

Widening her smile when the restraints were removed, she rose from the chair, trying to be graceful, but settling for steady.

"Of course, I'm excited. Aren't I supposed to be?" She spoke the words out loud, her tongue recovering faster than her fingers; or maybe it was because she'd been practicing them since receiving the draft notice. "Like the slogan says, I'm determined to be the RIGHT in the WORLD."

2

CHAPTER 2

8 DEC 2114

O UTSIDE WAS HOT. A dry heat that would burn your skin to a crisp if you weren't careful; an arid, earth-baking heat that the rain could only quench for that brief time right after a storm.

The ozone layer, according to a now-defunct scientific journal Kaalinda had read at her doctor's office, was now only a thin checkerboard of protection; the gray-green haze of pollution that hovered near the top of the atmosphere was thicker.

Kaalinda followed Johnson, her escort. He had nodded once when commanded to escort her to the next phase of selection, only grunting a reply to her soft "Hello".

The "next phase" was a medical exam and initial shots. This took place on the other side of the training facility. No transportation was provided for new recruits like Kaalinda. Maybe the journey in the heat was all part of her training.

She could see the capital in the distance, hidden under the large cloudy dome that offered protection from the searing heat and harmful rays that fell on the rest of the world. Inside, no one had to worry about the destructive elements of nature. Kaalinda had visited the capital often with her father. She let her thoughts wander through the museums and art galleries, still vivid in her mind.

She remembered her father's laugh, her mother's smile, strawberry ice cream melting as they walked in the manicured park, thesmell of sausage and mushroom pizza in "Uncle Chuck's Italian Ristorante".

She cut the thoughts off; remembering was not onher agenda for today. Wiping the few drops of water collecting in her eyes, she sniffed, rubbing her nose with the back of her hand, then rubbing her handalong the fabric of her pants leg.

Kaalinda struggled to keep up with Johnson's quick stride. Having never marched before, she was awkward, her steps unmatched. Johnson was very tall, more than a head taller than Kaalinda, and had a dark tan on his face and arms.

Drops of moisture zig-zagged their way down her cheeks and neck, pooling between her breasts and shoulder blades. They had only been outside for a couple of minutes.

Johnson seemed completely unaffected; Kaalinda couldn't see any sweat on him at all. Would she get used to the heat and humidity, the searing rays of sun that burnt plants to a crumbling husk on the farm?

The soldier marched in front, looking straight ahead, his chin pushed forward. His arms moved firmly at his sides, in rhythm with his legs. Kaalinda tried to mimic the motions, but she had to lunge her legs forward, and swing her arms high by her side, skipping every third step just to keep up.

When Johnson slowed his pace and shortened his stride, Kaalinda nearly plowed into the back of him. She caught herself, shortening her own stride, the movement becoming far more natural.

Johnson continued at the slower, shorter pace.

Kaalinda examined the back of his uniform. The jacket was neatly pressed, with three sharp, evenly spaced creases running down the length of the back. The creases became folds under the wide brown leather belt that encircled his waist. The sleeves were rolled up, creating a wide tight band around the upper part of his arms. Thick, rounded biceps were exposed, the muscles crisscrossed with prominent blue veins.

His trousers were of a camouflage print—green, brown, and black—to simulate dense foliage when seen from a distance. They were tucked into tall, tightly laced black combat boots, so highly polished they glared under the sun's rays. A brown leather pistol holster rested against his right thigh with a brown leather strap wrapped around the thigh to hold it in place. From what Kaalinda could see of the pistol inside, it was as highly polished as his boots. A stiffly starched camouflage cover, resembling a ball-cap, but much taller, offered a small degree of protection from the sun to his nearly shaven head.

It had been dark when her group had arrived yesterday, and the sun had not yet risen above the horizon when they had been rustled from their beds and herded into the bus for breakfast. Now, the sun high in the late morning sky, Kaalinda took the opportunity to examine her surroundings.

Swirls of silver-gray mist drifted upward from the ground. Frequent rain kept the ground moist, though there was as much pollution in the water that it did as much damage to the plant life as the sun and heat. Puddles of brownish water sat stagnant in the ditches, the metallic purple-blue-yellow of gasoline floating on top, strands of rotting material marring its sheen. The sun was already sucking the liquid back into the sky, returning the dirt to its arid bleakness. Black storm clouds formed on the horizon; the cycle would start all over again by noon.

Kaalinda inhaled, the thick polluted air catching in her lungs. She coughed, then tried to drag in more oxygen. It needs to rain again, she thought, rain would make it easier to breathe.

The cropped grass, tinged yellow from acid rain, tried to grow around the buildings. Sparse trees provided too little shade. Their near-barren limbs, the few leaves struggling to keep hold more orange than green, stretched up to the sky, begging for mercy from the unrelenting sun.

The crumbling flowerbeds that flanked the mainentrances to the buildings were empty. The bare earth already dry, the slight wind stirring dead leaves and dust into the air.

Concrete walkways were everywhere, crisscrossing lawns, joining entrances to buildings. Some had cracked surfaces jutting at odd angles, with deep crevices waiting to trip the unwary walker traversing their length. Others looked brand new, their pristine surfaces unmarred by foottraffic.

Drab green vehicles, dark smoke puffing from their exhausts, passed them, some transporting soldiers and some piled high with ammunition. Kaalinda could hear the uneven growl of an engine backfire, then, turn into a grumpy whine, as it strained under its cargo. The smell of gasoline and burning oil permeated the air.

Few people were outside alone.

Building number 27 was now in front of them. It was one story, built of drab slab concrete, with green carbonization stains running down the eroding surface of its walls. It was similar to every other building on the base except for the bright yellow number on the side. On the flat roof, black humps of tar emitted waves of heat into the blue-green sky above.

The tall, double doors were made of smoked glass; no finger smudges marred its surface. The brass trim gleamed where the sun's rays hit. Kaalinda could see the outline of a soldier who stood at parade rest just inside.

The silent guard held the door for Johnson and Kaalinda, letting them pass into the interior of the building. As soon as the door had closed, the soldier on watch snapped back to attention for a moment then moved to the door with a cloth in hand, and swiped away any dirt unwittingly placed on the glass.

Kaalinda had expected the building to be cool inside—but it wasn't. The smoky glass of the windows and doors kept some of the heat outside, but did nothing to combat the humidity.

She wrinkled her nose. The smell of mildew and bleach was pervasive. She could also smell burning wax and hear the dim whine of a floor buffer echoing through the passageways from some remote corner.

Johnson marched down the main corridor; Kaalinda followed, hardly daring to peek right or left.

Large wooden doors flanked either side. Ahead of them, Kaalinda noticed a black sign sticking out from the wall above one of the doors. Once they got close, she could read the yellowed lettering: NEWRECRUITS. The solder stopped in front of the door and motioned with his lefthand for her to enter.

A single, curt nod and he was gone.

Kaalinda stood outside the door for a moment, watching her escort stride away. Though she had just met him, hadn't even really spoken to him, she had formed an attachment to him. Now, alone, she felt bereft, uncertain. She wanted to cry.

Instead, she opened the door and stepped into the room. The harsh smell of bleach burned her nostrils and made her eyes water. She also thought she could smell alcohol and other medicinal smells she couldn't name.

It was a large room, without windows. Silent, dust-covered ventilation covers hung from the ceiling. The concrete block walls were painted white and seemed to glow beneath the glare of the fluorescent lights. A long row of molded orange plastic chairs sat against one wall and along counter, with a swing half-door, dividing the room. The counter had sides of simulated oak paneling, scratched and scarred, and a pale yellow top pockmarked and ink-stained. Past it, faded buff curtains separated three gurneys, all empty. Kaalinda could see faint blood stains on the nearest one.

Polished metal trays held an array of instruments and racks of different colored tubes. Metal carts held electronic gear and various other pieces of medical machinery Kaalinda didn't recognize.

White porcelain sinks, one with a black stain caused by a dripping faucet, were attached to the wall next to each gurney, their dusty copper pipes visible underneath.

A cabinet, made of the same materials as the counter, sat at the left of each sink. A set of metal canisters sat on each one, the labels faded and too far away for Kaalinda to read. A box of rubber gloves sat on the cabinet to the far right.

No one else was in the room. Sitting in one of the chairs, she waited. The monotonous drip of the leaky faucet was the only noise in the room.

There were no magazines, no posters on the walls, no eye charts or CPR instructions. Kaalinda couldn't even see a list of supplies to be kept in the cabinets. She examined the scratches in the paneling of the counter, playing a game, looking for patterns and shapes.

Kaalinda waited a long time, alone.

3

Chapter 3

8 Dec 2114

KAALINDA WAS ABSENTLY PICKING at a nub of fabric on her pant-leg when the door creaked open. She jumped up, snapping her body to attention.

A man, dressed in a blue lab coat, entered the room, looking at a piece of paper on a clipboard. He had a black pen tucked behind his left ear. Like the scientists at the machine, his streaky gray hair was cropped close, and his glasses, dangling by one stem from his mouth, were the same, wire-rimmed type. The lenses were thick though, for his eyes bulged when he placed them on his face to look at Kaalinda.

"Sit down." He had a deep voice, devoid of any accent or emotion. "So, you're it for this morning." It wasn't really a question.

Kaalinda stood, answering anyway, "Yes, Sir." Her own voice seemed strange, breathless.

"What's your name?"

Kaalinda cleared her throat. "Kaalinda Vesta MacReady, Sir." This time her voice sounded stronger, firmer.

Nodding, he motioned her through the half-door and onto one of the gurneys. "My name is Dr.

Samuel. I'll be performing some tests on you and giving you some shots."

Routine checks were done first – blood pressure, heart rate and body temperature. Kaalinda had seen similar units at her own doctor's office. This one looked older, its labels peeling and paint chipped. Dr. Samuel quietly explained that the test results were automatically downloaded into the mainframe computer and into her medical record. He left the unit running while he continued with the examination, listening to her lungs and checking her reflexes.

Taking a large needle from a metal tray resting on a table, Dr. Samuel checked it, then inserted it into Kaalinda's right arm. She felt a slight tingle as the serum entered her bloodstream. The puncture immediately began to itch. Kaalinda gritted her teeth. Knowing she couldn't touch her arm only made it worse.

"That was a biogenetic hormone injection. You will be receiving a booster about once a week during training. It will help your muscles develop stronger, faster. It should make your adjustment to military life easier."

Kaalinda nodded once again, trying to keep her eyes on what the doctor was doing, yet politely watch his face while he spoke.

He took another needle and attached it to a long piece of rubber tubing hooked to one of the machines on the cart. He then placed several tubes, each with a different colored stopper, into plastic casings in the machine.

With a soft humph and a nod, he reached for an elastic tourniquet. Kaalinda watched as he tied it around her upper left arm, stemming the flow of blood back to her heart. He examined the inside of her arm, prodding it with his forefinger, looking for a good vein. He then took the needle and placed it next to her arm. She closed her eyes as she felt the stab of the needle and its slow slide into her vein. She opened them again to watch the blood rush down the tubing as it was pumped from her body, spurting into the tubes of the apparatus.

Kaalinda wondered if she would have any blood left when her examination was done.

While the tubes were filling with blood, Dr. Samuel checked Kaalinda's blood pressure, ensuring that it did not drop too low.

"Beep."

A green light flashed on the blood pump. Dr. Samuel pulled the needle from Kaalinda's arm, applying pressure with a small piece of gauze. He took a small tube from the top drawer of the cabinet and removed the gauze, immediately squeezing a dab of clear gel over the puncture, thinning it out with one finger.

"Hold that arm still while this dries."

Dr. Samuel opened the cabinet drawer again, depositing the tube, then, opened the bottom door of the cabinet. He removed a blue power supply box and placed it atop the cabinet. Plugging it into a receptacle, he flipped a switch. A low hum indicated that it was now warming up.

Dr. Samuel removed the blood-pressure cuff from her arms, and the temperature probe from behind her ear. "Take your trousers and underwear off, please."

Kaalinda, pausing in a half-sitting position, wondered what was coming next.

"Hurry." Dr. Samuel was briskly scrubbing his hands at the sink, pink liquid soap becoming foamy white suds under the running tap.

Kaalinda stood, dropping her pants to the floor. They fell in a rumpled pile around her feet. Hooking her thumbs in the wide elastic waist of her white panties, she pushed them down to her ankles, balancing on her right leg to pull them off completely. She quickly folded the clothing, setting them in a small, neat pile next to the wall.

Her top was long enough to cover her to mid-thigh, but Kaalinda still felt exposed. No man, other than her father when changing her diapers, and her doctor in the reassuring presence of her mother, had ever seen that most private part of her body.

Kaalinda stood waiting, unsure. Was she to get back on the gurney?

Dr. Samuel finished scrubbing, and pulled on a new pair of plastic gloves. Patting the gurney with his left hand, he reached underneath to pull up the metal stirrups.

Swallowing hard past the lump that formed in her throat, Kaalinda slowly climbed back onto the gurney, and scooted her bottom down. She knew this routine. She kicked off her rubber flops and lifted her knees high, placing her heels in the cold stirrups. She scooted her bottom down a little more.

Dr. Samuel squeezed a clear jelly into the fingers of one hand, and moved to stand below her. Kaalinda stared up at the ceiling, noting a crack that started in one corner and ended at the light fixture hanging above her.

She closed her eyes when he inserted his cold, gooey finger, and tried to pretend that she was somewhere else, doing anything else. She tried to ignore the sharp pain when he pressed her abdomen with his other hand, moving that big, solid finger around inside.

The release of pressure was immense when he removed the finger. Kaalinda could feel the shift of urine into her bladder. She always had to urinate after an exam and could feel the drops of warm liquid escape her tense muscles.

She heard the metallic ting of the speculum being adjusted and tried to relax her pelvic muscles without expelling all the liquid.

The speculum was cold and hard against her tight muscles. She lost the battle with her bladder, and she felt the wet warmth against her bottom expand. She began to deepen her breaths, concentrating on that crack in the ceiling. She could feel the instrument slowly stretch her muscles,

"Okay, relax. I'm going to do the cervical scraping."

Relax? Kaalinda didn't think it was possible.

Just as Dr. Samuel picked up a long instrument, flat on the one end, Kaalinda heard the tell-tale creak of the main door opening. Dr. Samuel turned, and Kaalinda caught a glimpse of the shiny metal tool in his hand.

"Here's another recruit who passed, Doctor." Kaalinda could hear the voice, but could not see the speaker. The voice was deep and a bit raspy, like the speaker had a cold. Definitely a man, Kaalinda thought to herself.

"Good, good. Set him up next door." Dr. Samuel swept his right hand, still holding the metal instrument, toward the gurney next to them.

"Yes, Sir."

Kaalinda could hear the footsteps of two people: one in hard-soled shoes, the other in flip-flops. She could feel a red tide of color surge into her face, the heat of it burning her cheeks and neck.

The curtains were open, and the two people who had just entered the room could see her, see the polished shine of the speculum nestled between her parted legs.

Kaalinda heard the groaning protest of the other gurney as the recruit climbed atop it, and the bumps and thumps as the cabinets were opened and closed.

God, I hope that recruit couldn't see my face! Kaalinda allowed herself one vain thought. For just a moment, it distracted her from what was being done to her by the doctor.

Dr. Samuel turned back to Kaalinda, immediately inserting the scraping instrument, and obtaining the sample of cervix cells to be examined. Embarrassed by the thought of someone else seeing her, Kaalinda had no difficulty ignoring the scratching discomfort.

She started, however, when she heard the faint whine of a small motor. Looking to her right, she watched Dr. Samuel make adjustments at the blue power supply box he had removed from the cabinet. He attached a long flexible metal cable, with a wand at the tip. The very end of the wand glowed red.

Kaalinda could feel the fear rise from her stomach once again. She wanted to run - to jump off the gurney, pull out the speculum, and sprint for the door. Kaalinda moved slightly, edging her body closer to the edge of the gurney, when Dr. Samuel turned back around.

"Okay, we're almost done."

Kaalinda watched the doctor remove the speculum and toss it to the table, then pull down a large grey box on a long arm. It looked similar to the x-ray her dentist used, but the business-end lenses were pointing down.

Dr. Samuels positioned the box so that it hovered above her pelvis and pushed a button. It began to whir, and the two lenses swiveled, a faint, widish beam illuminating on her skin.

The contraption beeped and light flashed from the lenses.

A hot burning deep inside, one on each side of her pelvis, caused an involuntary shout of pain. The sharp sound echoed through the room.

"Could you feel that?" Dr. Samuel asked.

Tears streaming down her face, Kaalinda swallowed her sob and nodded. The salty wetness tracked to her lips, where a quick dart of the tongue removed it.

"Hmmm." Dr. Samuel pushed the contraption back to set against the wall, tapping the button to power it down. The soft whine disappeared.

"What did you do?" Kaalinda's voice was raspy and low.

Dr. Samuel, quickly removing the speculum didn't answer.

"Dr. Samuel?"

The doctor turned to Kaalinda, a slightly surprised expression covering his features. "We sterilize all recruits before training begins. Your ovaries were irradiated to stop ovulation." Dr. Samuel turned his back to her, removing his rubber gloves, then dropped them into a red container.

"You can get dressed now."

"Sterilized!?" Kaalinda couldn't name the emotion that filled her. It was part anger, part panic, part disbelief. It crashed through her like a tidal wave of ice. Kaalinda lay for a moment, unable to move. Her mind reeling from what had just happened, and the matter-of-fact delivery from Dr. Samuel.

"Sterilized?" This time the word was a strangled, choking whisper. Kaalinda had trouble controlling the movement of her tongue, and it seemed to fill her mouth as it formed the words, "I've been sterilized?"

Dr. Samuel lifted her legs from the stirrups, laying them on the gurney. "As I said, all recruits are sterilized before being released for training. I assume you did read all the disclosure forms?"

Disclosure forms? Kaalinda hadn't seen any disclosure forms, but wasn't given a chance to say so. She had never felt so helpless in her life. Not even when her family had died. Now, biting her lip, she choked back on her sob, and stared at the blurred image of the light above.

4

Chapter 4

8 Dec 2114

K AALINDA ROLLED TO HER left and stood, shaky legs struggling to keep her upright. She bent to retrieve her clothing, a faint twinge of pain in her abdomen reminding her of what had just happened. Two red areas of skin, slightly raised, evidenced where the radiation had been aimed. A thin trickle of blood trailed down her inner thigh, a warm wetness in the cold room.

She shook out her panties and pulled them on—backwards—she realized for they were tight in back and loose in front. She didn't bother correcting them. She quickly stepped into the pants, pulling them up, and tying the drawstring tight round her waist. Hastily, she shuffled her feet into the flip-flops, moving them from their haphazard positions at the end of the gurney.

From the corner of her right eye, Kaalinda watched Dr. Samuel pick up something from the tray that still rested next to the gurney. Watching how casually he stood, Kaalinda felt a hate churn in the pit of her stomach.

"I just need to tattoo the back of your head and we'll be done."

Another needle, Kaalinda thought, and lay back down on the gurney, this time on her stomach. The puddle of urine was cold as it seeped into the fabric that covered her thighs.

Placing one hand on the top of her head to steady it, Dr. Samuel began the process of tattooing her service number on the back of her head, just above the top of her neck. Kaalinda could feel every stick of the tiny needle, anticipation and tension making it torturous.

Large salty tears ran down her cheeks and pooled on the mattress, just beneath the spot where she rested her nose. Sterilized. The word and its full meaning began to sink in. Blue dye dripped wetly onto the cotton sheet, splotches hitting her sharply on the face and neck.

Kaalinda pressed her face into the softness of the well-worn cotton. Her hands were fisted tightly, grasping the cotton like a lifeline.

"Okay, we're done. You can get up now."

Her hands shaking, Kaalinda slowly released her grip on the cotton sheet, and lifted her head, blinking like an owl. The room seemed extraordinarily bright to her eyes. Unshed tears blurred the lights and objects around her.

Kaalinda staggered to her feet, grasping the edge of the gurney to steady herself. It rolled slightly beneath her weight. Her vision was blurry, the back of her head was on fire, and her stomach grumbled loudly, reminding her it was past time for lunch. Kaalinda refused to give into the desire of her body to faint.

Dr. Samuel jerked his head to his right. "Take this ticket with you. Wait outside for your escort."

The ticket was green, with 78432 printed on it in white: her service number. A line with Dr. Samuel's signature ran along one end. On the other end was a hole, with a knotted white string through it.

"You sterilized me?" Kaalinda couldn't stop herself from asking the question once more. She couldn't believe the procedure could be done so casually.

Dr. Samuel pursed his lips, irritation evident in his features. "I have answered this question twice already. I refuse to answer it again. Accept that it has been done and move on."

Kaalinda felt the sharp sting of anger tinge her cheeks red. Forgetting about the other recruit and the soldier behind the curtain, she lunged for Dr. Samuel, grabbing the collar of his shirt with both hands. She pulled her small frame to its full height, and pushed her face into his, nose to chin.

"You want me to move on? You just wiped out my dreams of a family, and you want me to move on?" Hysteria bubbled in her voice, making it squeak as she formed the words.

Dr. Samuel's face grew cold as he stared down at Kaalinda. "You are now in the CFoR. Your future belongs to the CFoR. Release your hold on me, or we'll have to sedate you." Dr. Samuel looked down at Kaalinda, his brows arching over his eyeglass frames.

Kaalinda curled her fingers into still talons and pounced.

Dr. Samuel, unsuspecting, fell to the floor, Kaalinda on top of him, the ragged ends of her shorn nails clawing at his face. Blood oozed from the scratches she made into his cheek.

"Argg!!!" Dr. Samuel yelled, raising his arms to cover his face. Kaalinda pummeled her fists into them. She made contact with his nose, causing more blood to spit out onto the floor.

Dr. Samuel continued to cry out, and the pounding of feet finally answered his painful summons.

Kaalinda was yanked back. Her fingers, grasping whatever they could, brought bits of fabric and hair with them. She felt a sharp prick in her arm, and then languid warmth began to fill her limbs.

"No-o-o!" The moan escaped Kaalinda's cracked lips. "No-o-o!" Softer this time "No-o-o..." She whispered, her lids sinking slowly over her eyes.

Through shuttered lids, Kaalinda noticed that a soldier now stood just behind Dr. Samuel, one had resting on his weapon. The weapon remained in its holster, but the holster was open, revealing the pistol inside.

The doctor who had entered earlier with the second recruit was wiping at Dr. Samuel's face with a white gauze, a gauze that was quickly staining red.

"No, no." Dr. Samuel waved the other doctor away from his face. "I'm fine Dr. Zamora."

A second soldier restrained Kaalinda, one muscular arm around her waist, the other under her left arm, with the forearm across her throat.

Kaalinda drew in a long, gasping breath. Slowly, her heartbeat calmed. The rush of hatred drained from her system, leaving her weak and exhausted.

"She had a biogenetic injection. It was probably just a reaction." Dr. Samuel continued his explanation to Dr. Zamora. "She went berserk in about half a second. Check her blood hormone levels." Dr. Samuel waved one blood-stained hand toward Kaalinda.

Dr. Zamora nodded, applying liquid bandage to Dr. Samuel's face. Impatient, Dr. Samuel grabbed the tube and applied the liquid himself, waving once more toward Kaalinda.

Dr. Zamora took the hint and grabbed a syringe and needle from the cabinet.

Kaalinda, lost in swirling lethargy, was oblivious to the needle and Dr. Zamora. Her eyes were closed, her breathing shallow and unsteady.

Placing the blood in the test unit, Dr. Zamora pressed a button then watched the small screen. Dr. Samuel, his glasses still lying crumpled and cracked on the floor, leaned toward the screen, squinting.

"Well? What does it say?" Dr. Samuel leaned even closer to the screen.

"You are correct, as usual. Her levels are way too high. There are dangerous amounts of adrenaline and testosterone in her blood." Dr. Zamora leaned back against the cabinet, crossing his arms in front of his chest. "We can assume that's what caused the attack, but I don't think we should take any unnecessary chances. We'll have to decrease her dosage by half for her future shots." Dr. Zamora glanced at Dr. Samuel. "Did you do her blood test before or after you gave her the shot?"

Stooping over a small keypad, Dr. Zamora typed instructions for Kaalinda's next shot. "There, that should do it." He turned to look at Dr. Samuel, brows raised, waiting.

Dr. Zamora looked up at Kaalinda, almost asleep now in the arms of the restraining soldier. "Release her. She's no longer a threat."

Dr. Samuel looked to Dr. Zamora, then, looked away.

"Yes, Sir." The soldier let her go.

Kaalinda almost fell to the floor when the soldier removed his arms. Catching herself by grasping the edge of the gurney, she stood, swaying. Her body sagged, her shoulders drooped, her head lolled forward.

Oh, God! How could they do this to me?

Weakly, Kaalinda pushed herself away from the gurney, and through the half-door in the counter, trudging to the door. Her feet dragged on the floor, the flip-flops sliding easily on the waxed tile. She had trouble grasping the doorknob. A weakness slowly invaded her fingers, spreading through her hands and up her arms.

The door seemed heavier than before; she wrenched it partly open and slid through the narrow slot.

Once outside, she let the door close heavily behind her, the loud click echoing in the quiet passageway. Leaning against the door, Kaalinda closed her eyes against the rippling floor beneath her feet. She could still feel the walls sway, so she moved carefully to her right, until she was leaning against the wall rather than the door, and sank down. Once she felt the coolness of the floor beneath her bottom, she let her legs fall open and her shoulders sag forward.

Her sobs filled the passageway. Racking sobs that rent through her entire body, making it shake and quiver. Hot tears scalded her cheeks, and she angrily wiped them away with one tightly balled fist.

Anger made her thinking fuzzy. She wanted to return to the examination room and tear Dr. Samuel apart.

Unfortunately, it did not give her the extra energy necessary to complete the take, and her legs buckled beneath her when she tried to stand. Helpless, she pounded her hands against the cool tile floor until they hurt.

"No!!" The word was ripped from her lips. "Noooo...."The word turned into a keening wail that echoed down the passage.

Kaalinda listened as it whispered away.

Finally, exhaustion claimed her body and it went limp, becoming part of the wall. Her red, wet face turned toward the wall, looking for a place to rest.

She fell asleep waiting for her escort.

5

CHAPTER 5

8 DEC 2114

A ROUGH HAND ON her shoulder woke Kaalinda.

Blinking, she tried to focus on the pair of green figures looming over her.

"Are you MacReady?"

Frowning, Kaalinda nodded, scrambling her hands against the concrete wall behind her, trying to push herself to her feet.

One of the figures bent to pull her to her feet, lifting her off the ground. Her head slammed into the wall behind her.

"You're going to the brig."

"Hunh?" Kaalinda squinted at the two men, focusing on their faces. Both wore sneers, their teeth appearing pointed between their parted lips.

Flanked by the two soldiers, Kaalinda stumbled forward. Each man held one arm, pulling her along so that she walked on her toes .

The sudden glare of the sun after the dimness of indoors blinded Kaalinda. She tripped over her feet, one of the soldiers jerking her back up, his hands bruising her upper arm.

Kaalinda flinched but remained silent.

The brig was situated in an old bunker once used for ammunition storage. It had been built on the edge of the base and surrounded by 10-foot-high electric fences. The fence was now half fallen, the electricity long shut off. The gates were left permanently open. An old generator whined, providing the only source of energy for the lights.

Kaalinda was led through a low door at one end of the bunker. Inside, the light was dim, the florescent lights flickering from the uncertain electric flow.

A long, narrow hall stretched the length of the bunker, metal mesh doors lining each side. The cells were only six feet high, by six feet wide, by six feet deep. No light was provided inside the cell, save for the slight trickle that leaked in from the hall.

The MP chose one of the doors, tapped a code into the electronic padlock, and then swung open the door. He pushed Kaalinda down and through the opening.

Inside, Kaalinda looked around. It was hard to see. Everything appeared as gray outlines against black.

There was no cot, no blanket, and no pillow. A bucket in the corner served as a toilet.

Kaalinda sank into the far corner, away from the door. It was cold. She could feel her breath freezing in front of her face, even though she couldn't see the frozen mist.

Huddling against the wall, Kaalinda wrapped her arms around herself, the tears beginning to flow. No one heard her soft sobs, or her whispered question "Why?".

***

Not sure of how long had passed, Kalinga woke. The floor of her cell was cold beneath her body where she lay, its dirt surface damp and moldy. Pebbles imprinted themselves into the soft flesh of her stomach.

She rested her head on folded arms, staring into a dark corner. The tears had run out long ago.

Still no blanket, no pillow. No toilet, and she couldn't force herself to urinate over the tiny bucket in the corner. It had a hole in the bottom, where the seam had rusted through. Using the bucket would be the same as just squatting in the corner.

Kaalinda wondered if she could hold the urine in her bladder much longer. Cramps had started after the last guard had passed. She wasn't sure how long ago that had been.

Time. The concept seemed far away at that moment. Her arrival at the base seemed so long ago, yet Kaalinda knew it had only been yesterday. At least, she thought it was yesterday.

She didn't think she had spent an entire day in the brig yet. She couldn't be positive, though. There was no light from the outside reaching her confines, so she had no indication of the time of day.

A faint, off-key hum reached her ears.

The guard!

Maybe he would be in a better mood. Maybe the watch had changed, and this was a different guard, one who would lead her to a toilet.

Slowly, careful of her cramping muscles, Kaalinda sat up. Holding her breath, she listened to the approaching soldier.

No.

It was the same tune as before. It became louder, mixing with the shuffling of boots along the loose dirt of the corridor floor.

Kaalinda tensed.

It stopped outside the door to her cell.

She jumped as the door rattled against its hinges. The guard kicked the door again.

"You awake in there?"

"Yes." Kaalinda answered, moving away from the door on hands and knees, crouching in the far corner.

"You still need to piss?"

The guard's voice was muffled, possibly slurred.

"Yes." Kaalinda pushed herself even farther into the corner.

"Wanna make a deal?"

She held her breath. The door swung open, light flooding the floor. It didn't reach her corner hideaway, and Kaalinda kept still, waiting.

"Come on out." The guard waved one hand and arm, nearly unbalancing himself in the process. "I'm having a little party, and I'm inviting you."

Kaalinda remained still, watching.

The guard shook his finger in the general direction of the cell. "Don't make me come in there after you."

Licking dry lips, Kaalinda slowly pushed herself to her feet. Keeping her eyes on the weaving guard, she moved into the light, blinking.

"Can I use the toilet?"

"Sure, sweetie, just follow me."

The guard moved back for her to walk ahead of him down the corridor. Keeping as far from him as she could, Kaalinda left her cell.

The smell of alcohol was enough to make her head spin. The guard was drunk.

Dread wound through Kaalinda's stomach, and her breathing sped up. She felt like a mouse caught in a mousetrap, with the cat stalking her from behind.

The guard resumed his whistling, a perverse tune Kaalinda recognized from university get-togethers, about chickens and whips. Kaalinda forgot about the large quantity of urine demanding release from her bladder.

The duty office was a small room near the entrance to the brig. A wooden door, scratched and dented, offered privacy for napping and eating. A small toilet and sink were nestled behind a half-wall in one corner.

A wooden desk held a radio and a flashlight. A map of the brig, under Plexiglas, was mounted on the wall. Small dots, stuck to the glass, indicated which cells held prisoners. Kaalinda counted over 15 before the guard nudged her toward the corner.

Turning, Kaalinda scanned the guard once more. His uniform was wrinkled and food stains dotted the front of his shirt.

"Are you going to wait outside?" Kaalinda thought she knew what his answer would be.

"Now, why should I do that? We're going to have us a little party. Remember?"

He pulled the door shut behind him, then walked to the desk, tugging at a wide drawer in the desk. It opened on his third yank on the handle, revealing several bottles. He pulled one out, offering it to Kaalinda.

Kaalinda shook her head. "No, thank you."

Shrugging, the guard opened the top, putting it to his lips for a long drain of the liquid inside, keeping his glazed stare on Kaalinda. Once finished, he smacked his lips, wiping them with his sleeve.

Swallowing hard, Kaalinda retreated to the corner, thankful for the half-wall of privacy. Her bladder was once again reminding her of the immediate problem.

Keeping a watchful eye on the guard, she turned her back to the toilet, then, pushed down her pants. The seat was cold.

She breathed a sigh of relief as the warm liquid exited her body. Her muscles pushed hard against her bladder, trying to release the liquid as quickly as she could. She wanted to finish before the guard made his move.

Sitting, the wall obscured her view of the room, and the guard. Kaalinda listened for his boots on the floor.

Unfortunately, the floor of the duty office was carpeted.

Kaalinda was pulling up her pants, not bothering to wipe with the scratchy CFoR-issued tissue, when the guard approached...and was confronted headlong with a very hard reminder that she was a small woman alone with a very large man.

The guard had opened his trousers and undershorts, dropping them to below his knees. His left hand fondled his erect penis; his right hand stroked his stubble-covered chin.

"Are we ready to party?"

Kaalinda froze, staring at the long, dusky pink member jerking mere inches from her nose. It shone in the fluorescent light, semen oozing from its tip.

She forced her eyes upward, to the face of the guard who now seemed to tower above her. His face was shadowed, his head outlined by the light directly behind it. He was like a menacing reaper from a childhood nightmare.

He thrust his hips forward, twice. "Come on, baby. I'm sure you know what to do with my friend. You look like you've done this before."

Kaalinda stared a moment longer. Time seemed frozen. Her mind struggled to grasp what was happening, to reach a conclusion and action.

The guard licked his lips. "Let's try it in the mouth first."

He lunged forward, his right hand grabbing her shirt, pulling it up. His left hand slipped under the material, moving up to her breast, squeezing when it found its target.

Kaalinda gasped, struggling for release.

"Ooh, I like a girl who resists."

Sobbing, Kaalinda tried to pull herself free. He pinched her nipple in retaliation, his right hand now pushing at her pants.

When his fingers slipped between her legs, thrusting roughly, a rage crashed through her. Violent heat thawed the ice that held her body and brain frozen, and she moved.

Her knee drove upward, slamming into his groin, crushing his member into the hard muscle of his thigh.

The guard bellowed, his hands releasing her.

Kaalinda's breast throbbed. She ignored the pain, following her first movement with a second. This time, her hands pushed down on the back of his head, driving it into the wall behind the toilet, twisting her body to the side.

His head cracked as it hit the wall, blood spurting out into the toilet, turning the yellowed water in its basin to orange, then to red.

Kaalinda backed away, stumbling over his boot clad feet. Staring at the fallen soldier, Kaalinda sobbed once more, her hands covering her face, the skin burning in reaction.

Glancing around the room, Kaalinda spied the open liquor bottle setting on the desk. Picking up the guard's cover, she used it to keep her fingerprints from the bottle, which she tossed to the floor next to the guard.

The remaining liquid bubbled from it, pooling on the floor, wetting the material of his trousers.

Turning, Kaalinda dropped the cover and ran down the dim corridor, ducking into her cell, the door still hanging open. Pulling the door closed behind her, she heard the low click of the lock.

She was once more safely locked in her cell.

6

CHAPTER 6

9 DEC 2114

KAALINDA'S EYES FELT DRY and scratchy, like shards of shrapnel had scored them sometime through her sleepless night. Dried tears caked in the creases around her eyes and in her eyelashes, sticking them together.

Her fits of dozing had been cut short by nightmares. In her dreams, she had not escaped the guard last night, but was left here forever, locked in the brig, "partying" every night.

She awakened each time, feeling his hands on her breast, between her legs, his penis pushing into her mouth. Gagging dry heaves leaving her spent and drained, she had shrunk back into her corner each time, praying for someone to come release her.

Now, huddled into the corner, listening to the dark silence that engulfed her cell, she was not certain when she had realized she was the solitary prisoner at the brig, but she had felt interminably alone ever since.

Fear that she would be forgotten here, to starve and die, fought with the relief that she would not have to deal with the guard. The war was currently at an impasse.

The scrape of metal door on dirt caught her unawares, and Kaalinda screamed, before she reminded herself that she had killed the guard. It couldn't be the soldier whose ghost had tormented her all night.

"Hey, hey...it's okay." A soothing voice stretched into the darkness, reaching her in the corner, squelching her scream. "I've come to take you back to medical."

Gasping, Kaalinda struggled to pull air into her lungs, to calm her rapid breathing.

The soldier squatting in the doorway, framed by the golden light from the lamps in the hall, seemed familiar somehow, his voice ringing true to Kaalinda's ears. He held out one hand, offering her escape from the darkness.

She stared at the extended hand. The light from the corridor falling on the upheld palm made it seem surreal. Crawling forward, hesitant, she stopped just outside an arm's reach of his hand. Studying it, Kaalinda noticed the lines on the palm, the calluses on the fingertips, the flesh stretched taut over long, slender fingers.

He extended it further, and she was pulled to her feet and led out of the cell. The soldier closed the door to the cell, careful to keep it from slamming, pausing to let her eyes adjust to the bright light of the hall.

Kaalinda stood in the light, feeling it on her face. It was like water on dry skin, and she absorbed it, momentarily closing her eyes.

Awareness of being watched made her open them. She looked first at her escort, then down the hall toward the duty office. She could hear low whispers leaking up the long corridor.

Her savior stood tall and silent beside her, his hands clasped behind him.

Taking a deep breath, Kaalinda noticed an odd smell. Wrinkling her nose, she turned back to her escort, eyeing his dark green uniform, sharp pleats crisscrossing it in odd directions.

He grimaced, shrugging his broad shoulders, beneath a wrinkled green jacket. "It's new. Issued to me just yesterday. I'm in your battalion."

Kaalinda looked up, only now noticing his freshly shaven head, red scratches indicating where he had been cut during the procedure. His skin was dark, other than the pale part on the top of his head. His eyes were a deep teal above a long, straight nose. Full, wide lips filled the space beneath his nose, leading to a strong, aquiline jaw.

Laughter from the duty office drew Kaalinda's attention once more. Her stomach tightened, the knots growing in size and strength.

"Hey, are you okay?" Her escort spoke in those same gentle tones, laying one hand on her shoulder.

Kaalinda flinched, instinctively moving away from his touch. Her back bumped the wall, and she looked up.

Take it easy girl, he's not going to hurt you. He's not that drunken guard trying to rape you. This Kaalinda said to herself; to her escort she said, "I'm sorry." Her voice was low and raspy.

"Hey. It's okay." He held his hands up. "Let's just get out of here. I can understand why one night in this place would spook you." He nodded toward the sounds emitted from the duty office. "The two MPs sent me down here to get you. They went in to talk to the guard."

"Hey! Recruit!" A voice shouted from the duty office. "You get her out?"

"Yes, Sir!" He responded just as loud, the clipped words echoing down the lengthy corridor.

"Get up here then. We wanna talk to 'er."

Kaalinda felt the blood in her body drain to her feet, and she swayed, placing one hand against the wall to steady herself.

"Yes, Sir!" Kaalinda's escort indicated that she precede him.

Swallowing hard, Kaalinda moved forward, her flip-flops making a rustle-flap noise. She trailed one hand along the wall, its cool concrete surface a rough reality in an otherwise unreal maze.

"Oh, by the way, I'm Ramirez." His voice came from just above her left shoulder.

Kaalinda nodded. "Nice to meet you." The pleasantry was flat, without inflection. A faded image of her mother, lecturing her on the merits of always being polite appeared in Kaalinda's mind. Quirking her lips to the right, she considered those instructions now.

Somehow, I don't think Mother meant a situation like this.

She slowed her pace as they neared the duty office. The smell of alcohol was strong. Kaalinda choked back a gag, the spasm almost doubling her over with its force. She placed a hand over her nose.

Ramirez held her arm, offering support.

"Hey, what's taking you so long?" A soldier appeared in the doorway, a gold-colored badge pinned to his left breast pocket and collar insignias indicating he was an MP officer. Frowning, he nodded toward Kaalinda, who as now leaning into Ramirez. "What's with her?"

"She started gagging when she smelled the alcohol. Dr. Samuel said she had a shot yesterday that she reacted to." Ramirez shrugged. "Or maybe she's just real sensitive to smell."

Kaalinda stood up. Her face was pale and peppered with drops of sweat. Drool slipped form the corner of her mouth. She wiped it away with the back of her hand. She breathed through her mouth, drawing in large amounts of air, slowly. It helped.

"I'm sorry officer. I haven't eaten since yesterday." *Please don't ask me any questions. Please.*

The officer frowned, thick black brows meeting over dark brown eyes. "Think you'll be okay for a couple of minutes here?"

Swallowing the bile rising in her throat, Kaalinda nodded.

"You been here all night, right?"

Kaalinda nodded again.

The officer pushed his bottom lip out and cocked his head to one side, observing Kaalinda for a moment before speaking again.

"What did-j-you hear?"

Kaalinda licked her lips, clasping her hands in front of her. She stared at his badge when she gave him her answer. "Mostly just the guard humming when on rounds. He always banged on my door when he passed; he sounded pretty drunk."

"Do you know when he last made a round?"

Kaalinda lifted her eyes to the officer's face, looking him square in the eyes. "I'm not even sure what time it is now."

The officer nodded, leaning back against the doorjamb.

Kaalinda caught a glimpse into the duty office when he moved. The second officer was pulling the guard away from the toilet. Blood soaked the man's uniform, staining it dark brown. A soft whimper escaped her lips.

"My God!" Ramirez spoke from behind her, leaning forward so his breath brushed against Kaalinda's ear. He placed his hand on her shoulder, pushing her to one side for a better view.

The officer turned his gaze to the room. "Seems he got drunk and fell while pissin' in the john. There's enough liquor in here to get a battalion shit-faced." The officer shook his head. "Shame really. They were getting ready to transfer him outta this job."

Kaalinda looked around the room. The officers had pulled the bottles from the desk, and set them in a row on top, full ones to the left, the empties to the right.

"Go ahead and get her over to medical. You 'member the way?" The officer paused in the act of straightening from the doorjamb, palms resting on his thighs.

Ramirez nodded, taking Kaalinda's arm to lead her away.

Kaalinda let him pull her along, her steps automatic. She couldn't stop staring at the corpse in the duty office. Memories of her previous visit to the room returned, and Kaalinda shook her head to clear it.

"It's okay, MacReady. I don't think you'll be coming back here. I overheard Dr. Samuel getting screamed at for not checking your blood counts before giving you that shot. Seems the whole thing could have been avoided if he had checked for a proper dosage."

Kaalinda looked up into Ramirez' face, and it struck her once more that he looked familiar. His voice was familiar. But she still couldn't remember where she might have seen him.

Her stomach rumbled, the acids violently protesting their lack of action.

Ramirez laughed. "Let's get you to Dr. Samuel before you die of starvation. Then, we'll get you some breakfast."

Kaalinda tried to smile, but couldn't find it in herself to be happy to be going back to medical.

She thought about the injection. It was the hormone that had given her the surge of adrenaline needed to defeat the drunken guard. So...a part of her was happy the doctor had botched the dosage.

Of course, another voice whispered inside her head, if he hadn't botched the dose, you never would have been sent to the brig in the first place.

Confused and tired, Kaalinda followed the blurry back of her battalion-mate. Boot camp wasn't much like the brochures.

7

CHAPTER 7

10 DEC 2114

STIFLING HER YAWN, KAALINDA blinked twice, trying to keep her eyes open. Her eyes were dry and bloodshot from a short night's sleep, and the tears her lids applied to their surface made them burn.

Her mouth tasted like what Kaalinda imagined a decaying rat might taste like. A viscous, putrid mucus had formed at the top of her throat, and no amount of spitting or toothpaste had removed it.

Her teeth, when touched by her tongue, were covered in a gritty residue her toothpaste had been unable to remove. The faint mint taste of the green paste had not been much against the horrible taste either.

Her body smelled faintly of sweat. The quick two-minute shower she had been allowed that morning had not quite done its job. She had no soap or washcloth yet. They would be issued later in the day.

Just three days ago, Kaalinda had been at the machine, then through that horrible nightmare of a medical exam.

Kaalinda still worried that charges would be laid against her attack on the doctor. They had simply released her after her one night in the brig, letting her continue as if nothing had happened. Kaalinda felt like she was being watched, but she couldn't see who was watching. Some of her battalion-mates talked about her; she heard the whispers that stopped when she got close and saw the looks of contempt in their eyes.

A little girl inside wanted to go home.

Pushing those thoughts away, she peeked around the recruit in front of her to see ahead.

A long line of recruits stretched in front of her, moving ahead rather quickly through the chow line. The mess hall was massive and crammed from wall to wall with tables, presently full of eating recruits. They shoveled the food into their mouths with fingers and utensils, bits falling to their plates in their haste.

Kaalinda swallowed the bile that rose from her stomach at the smell of meat and sweat and burnt grease. She wondered how anyone could eat with such a smell in the air.

The line moved forward, the recruit at the front taking a metal tray from the stack, then moving on to the food.

A large glass window, steam condensing on its surface, separated the recruits from the warming trays. Heat lamps were set up to keep it warm.

Recruits, dressed in white food service aprons and jackets, served the food, dumping ladles of unrecognizable mush onto plates for the recruits in line to eat. Sweat beaded on the foreheads of the servers. Kaalinda tried not to notice when drops of it landed in the food.

Placing her tray on the metal guides, Kaalinda gave her choices to the server—scrambled eggs, hash browns, and toast.

The food was placed on the plate, then, handed across the top of the glass counter to Kaalinda. Taking the plate, she quickly moved it to her tray as the heat of it burned her hand. Glancing at the recruit who had given it to her, she caught the smug half-grin he didn't bother hiding.

Kaalinda felt the surge of anger sweep through her, burning in her gut. The nausea in her stomach vanished. Her weariness disappeared. A red tide of rage laid siege to her brain. Riding it was a small amount of fear, a fear that she was quickly losing control of herself.

A jostle from the recruit behind her brought her back to the moment. The tide receded. Kaalinda took a deep breath, her stomach once again roiling against the odor.

Kaalinda moved on, the recruits behind her continuing to push her forward.

A tray of glasses already containing milk was set on a table near the end of the line, as well as a precarious stack of bowls and boxes of dry cereal.

"Just two." The server behind the table spoke to Kaalinda without looking at her, he was busy filling two glasses with milk from a dispenser at the same time. Kaalinda chose two from the back. The coolness of the glass reassuring.

She also chose a box of cereal and a bowl, and picked up her utensils, riffling through the containers to find ones without dried pieces of food stuck to them.

Turning to the roomful of recruits, she searched for the rest of her group. Seeing them at a table near the corner, she walked toward them, careful not to spill anything on her tray.

The noise was harsh to her ears. There was no rumble of voices, just the clank of metal trays, the scrape of chair legs, and the grate of fork against plate. It was enough to give her a toothache.

Sitting with her group, Kaalinda looked at the food on her plate. She couldn't discern which was the scrambled egg and which were the hash browns—they were both a gray, lumpy mass.

Picking up her fork, she placed a tiny bit in her mouth. Kaalinda tried to swallow, but the food had lodged in her throat and wouldn't pass any farther. She spit the offending lump into her paper napkin. Her stomach growled. Taking a deep breath, Kaalinda sniffed one of the two glasses of milk she had been given. It smelled okay.

Kaalinda tried a small sip, letting her tongue touch the cool liquid first. It tasted okay.

Downing the glass stopped her stomach growling.

Kaalinda looked at the plate of food she had been given. What she now thought were the eggs were runny and tasted odd. The toast was black and cold. She opened the box of whole bran cereal and poured it into a small bowl. Her second glass of milk was poured over that.

She finished her breakfast well within the 15-minute time limit her small group had been given.

Sitting quietly in the plastic, orange chair, Kaalinda glanced at the others in her group.

She was the only female.

She was the shortest.

And from the conversation she had so far overheard, she was also the smartest.

Ramirez seemed to be the oldest—though not by much, he could be but maybe three years her senior—and had taken charge of the group. He had taken upon himself the task of organizing them into a squad when marching, giving them directions and delegating the tasks assigned by their escort. Soon, they would be formed into an actual battalion, with instructors and recruit leaders. The just needed to wait for enough recruits to pass the machine.

Ramirez stood about six feet tall, about the average height for the men in the group. His eyes were still the bright teal she remembered from the brig, and the bits of stubble left on his chin were black.

Turner was the tallest in the group, standing half a foot taller than Ramirez. He had cut himself a couple of times with his dull razor, and the small red dots were covered with tissue.

Kaalinda thought Turner was probably blond. He had pale skin and pale blue eyes. He was thin, with narrow shoulders and long gangly limbs. He walked a bit stooped, his head bowed forward.

She didn't much like the rest of the group. One recruit mumbled when he talked, and they still weren't sure of his name. The others were downright rude to Kaalinda, ignoring her pleasantries and offering "comments" on her female form.

Those comments...she didn't dare admit they made her uncomfortable. She was here to become tough, to become one of the guys. She needed to ignore them as much as they were now ignoring her.

She watched the recruits sitting at the other tables eat. Those in the solid green uniforms, designating them as full recruits-in-training, were far more enthusiastic than those in the pale blue cotton suits.

The new recruits wore a uniform of pale blue scrubs and flip-flops. A letter designated each group of twenty; a number identified each individual. The letter/number combination was stenciled on the back of the shirts they wore.

Kaalinda's shirt had G-10 on the back.

Very few women sat at the tables. Those that did were very tall and very muscular—physiques very different from Kaalinda's.

Briefly, Kaalinda wondered if there had been some mistake made when she had been drafted, then remembered Dr. Samuel's comment after her shot. It had been something that would make her develop stronger muscles.

Kaalinda glanced at a tall, broad-shouldered female sitting two tables down, busily shoveling brown mush into her mouth. The recruit was taller than the men sitting on either side of her. Had the shot had made the woman look like that?

Somehow, though, Kaalinda didn't think that shot would make her grow any taller than she already was.

Their escort arrived, wearing a gray dress uniform, shiny medals dangling over his left pocket. He was clean-shaven, though a tinge of dark shadow could be seen beneath his chin.

He was the senior officer destined to be one of the Battalion Commanders. Black letters on a gold tag read DENISON.

Major Denison now stood at the end of their table. Somehow understanding what was expected, the group put their utensils, and swallowed what food was in their mouths.

Satisfied, Major Denison, nodded. "Atten-hutt!"

The group instantly stood, pushing their chairs back all at once. The harsh scraping of metal against tile giving Kaalinda goose bumps.

"Pick up your trays. Form one line, single file, to that window." Major Denison pointed to a window in the far wall, where white uniformed recruits could be seen scrubbing at trays and pans. Steam escaping from the hole to pool against the ceiling. The tiles there were marked by the green of mildew.

Kaalinda picked up her tray and led the rest of the group to the window. They quickly fell in behind her, and to her right. Since she was shortest, the group marked their stride off hers. Major Denison stood to the right of the window, watching.

The group formed into a loosely formed squad, four across, to wait. Ramirez stood near the front, facing the group, ready to lead their march back to their quarters.

8

CHAPTER 8

14 DEC 2114

KAALINDA LAY STILL.

She ignored the loud, sharp notes of reveille that caused her ears to cringe in protest.

Every muscle in her body was frozen. The smallest notion she took to move caused pain. Excruciating pain that lashed at her body, causing the muscles to knot into tight balls of fire. The muscles in her thighs and calves burned even while she lay still. It seemed that even the blood that surged through her veins hurt. *Maybe the pain would ease if she stopped breathing?*

Kaalinda took a deep breath, the pain as her chest moved made her whoosh it back out. She breathed more shallowly on her second attempt, holding her mouth and nostrils closed, trapping the air deep within her lungs for a moment before letting it out.

She was in good physical condition. She had thought the grueling pace she had pushed her body to maintain—the daily runs, sit-ups and pushups until she collapsed—would have prepared her for this. But it hadn't even come close.

Yesterday, they had run all day—in their combat boots, full uniform, and loaded backpacks. The hard, nearly inflexible reinforced canvas of the boots had caused large, pus-oozing blisters to form on the soles of her feet, and the skin on the tips of her toes to rub and burn. The sweltering heat had caused her head to swim, her eyes to lose focus. The sour water in their canteens had been all they had to drink.

They hadn't even stopped to eat, but kept running, stuffing dry bread and meat into their mouths, pulling their rations awkwardly from the heavy packs they carried on their backs. Kaalinda had been unable to keep her meal down, the recruits behind her pushing her along as she bent over, the contents of her stomach splashing against the dry, dusty dirt of the road.

The company that had staggered into their compartment last evening had been a mess. Kaalinda recalled the smell of sweat, blood, and burned flesh mixing and spreading through the room, and her stomach rolled at the memory. She remembered the moans of pain as socks, the caked blood sticking them to the flesh, were pulled off. Kaalinda's stomach convulsed. The putrid smell of infection still lingered in the stale air of the chamber.

The burned skin on faces, necks, and arms caused cries of distress as the hard surge of water from the showers hit it. Sweat and heat rash covered the backs of knees and under arms.

Kaalinda had taken her ration of fresh bandages and first aid ointment to a corner, removing herself from the others. Her tears had been for her alone.

Once she had carefully wrapped her feet, their swollen tissue thrumming with the pulse of blood, she had dried her face, careful of the tender skin there, and crawled to her rack. Kaalinda had navigated through the unconscious bodies of comrades, who, unable to gain the relative comfort of their top racks, were sprawled on the cool floor. She was grateful her rack was on the bottom.

She had thought—prayed—last night that she would dic.

But she was not that lucky, and now lay stiff in her rack, unable to move.

Oh, she knew she would have to move eventually. The commanders would come drag her out by her feet as a last resort, hoisting her body onto the backs of the other recruits in her company.

"Hey, MacReady?" It was the voice of Recruit Battalion Commanding Officer Wilkins. A hand reached out to shake her. She winced, pain shooting through her shoulder, arm, and back, but said nothing, keeping her eyes closed.

"Wake up. It's time to get moving."

Kaalinda kept her eyes closed, ignoring the urgent whispers around her. She could hear shuffling noises, but paid no attention to them.

Then...hands grasped her feet and she was pulled to the floor, her blanket covering her face. The first kick came as a surprise. The second made her angry.

The third kick never made contact with her body.

Quickly, surprising even herself, she grabbed the foot, encased in the hard, black leather combat boot, and yanked. The owner of the foot fell sharply. The crack of his head hitting the brown tile of the floor was like a crack of thunder, ominous and over in an instant.

Struggling to drag the blanket from her face, Kaalinda surged to her knees, ignoring the pain in her muscles. Her breathing stopped. Before her, on the cold tile floor, lay the recruit who had kicked her.

Unconscious, Recruit Commander Wilkins lay pale and unmoving. Ramirez was already at his side, checking for a pulse.

Kaalinda watched Ramirez carefully, letting out her pent-up breath when she saw him relax, his head hanging to rest his chin against his chest.

She felt numb. The pain in her muscles evaporated the instant she felt the first kick, adrenaline chasing away the stiffness. Her brain felt numb, as well. It couldn't seem to form a thought.

Function slowly returned to her muscles and brain. She stood, in slow motion, not quite trusting her legs. Shakily, they held her body up.

She balled up the blanket, throwing it carelessly onto her rack, one corner drooping to the floor. She took a deep breath and assessed the situation.

Hardening her features, she grabbed the arm of Carter, dragging his attention away from Wilkins and Ramirez.

"What the hell were you doing?"

Carter backed away from the anger emanating from Kaalinda. "It was his idea." Carter jerked his head toward Wilkins.

Ramirez looked up, glancing first at Kaalinda, then at Carter. Kaalinda noted the movement, but did not look at him.

Carter began to shake his head.

Ramirez spoke then, his voice deep and liquid. "Carter, what was going on?"

"Wilkins said he had permission to do whatever was necessary to keep MacReady in line. He's been looking for an excuse to do something to her." Carter glanced down at the still figure of the recruit BCO. "He was really looking forward to it."

Ramirez stood. "Did he specifically say he had permission to do this to MacReady, or was it any recruit?"

Carter licked his lips, avoiding the gaze of both Kaalinda and Ramirez, gazing instead at the beige wall of the compartment. Finally, whispering, "He said MacReady."

Ramirez took charge then, calling to the rest of the company. "Get on with the morning routine. Get in uniform then stand for a quick inspection." He glanced down at Wilkins. "Watch! Call for a medic!"

Somehow, Kaalinda remained calm and got dressed, making her bunk without thinking about the steps of the process—like an automaton.

She didn't watch the medical team arrive; she did watch them dump their equipment on the floor in front of Wilkins.

They were silent, seeming to communicate with each other without words. The watch, pale, his hand resting on the pistol in the holster, kept eyeing Kaalinda.

She ignored him, too.

Kaalinda ignored everyone.

On her way to the head, wash cloth in hand, she had to move around the still unconscious body, and did so without looking down. With measured steps, she walked to the head, ducking quickly into the row of toilet stalls. She chose the stall at the end, closing the door softly behind her.

Alone in the stall, washcloth crushed in her hands and stuffed to her mouth, knuckles white, Kaalinda choked out muffled sobs.

The rest of her battalion let her be.

Once the tears stopped, Kaalinda felt in control, and the numbness crept back into her mind and body. She let it come, preferring it to the wracking sobs that made her lungs and stomach hurt. Wilkins wasn't worth crying over.

9

CHAPTER 9

14 DEC 2114

BREAKFAST, CONSISTING OF GRITS, soft bacon, and biscuits—all of it greasy—was eaten without noticing its taste, or rather the lack of taste. Kaalinda felt the eyes of her fellow recruits upon her, knew that she should feel some degree of discomfort, but found that she couldn't. Her emotions were locked away inside and she couldn't find the key to let them out. The others tossed wary glances in her direction, pausing with their food halfway to their mouths.

After chow, they ran.

A paved track, with faint white lines indicating where they were supposed to run, lay on the outskirts of the training facility. It was here that the battalions performed calisthenics and exercises each morning, before they trained in basic military procedures.

This morning, Kaalinda ran fast. Her brain didn't pay attention to her body, and the stiffness and pain that normally slowed her down seemed nonexistent. The battalion, used to the slower pace she usually set, lagged, expecting her to drop out at any minute.

But Kaalinda kept running. At the final lap, she passed the battalion still running in formation. Kaalinda didn't care that she had broken rank, that she could be punished, probably by running even more laps. It just didn't matter right now.

"MacReady!" Ramirez' shout brought her to a halt. She turned to face her senior recruit.

"What are you doing?"

"Running."

"You've finished your laps. Walk it off."

Kaalinda stood for a moment, breathing heavy, and the blood pounding in her legs.

"Ramirez?" She was gasping.

The recruit turned back to her, one eyebrow raised in question.

"I'd rather keep running 'til the others are done."

Ramirez stared at her for a silent moment, then, nodded. "Don't overdo it. Denison will be mad as hell if you run out of steam in the maze today."

Kaalinda nodded, then, started running again. She sprinted hard, like hounds were chasing her, nipping at her heels. The hounds of hell; Cerebus and his whole family.

Kaalinda began to pass the battalion once again. She ran to the outside, legs pumping, arms keeping time, her brain whizzing along at light speed, but still trapped in the blanket from this morning.

She didn't see the foot that kicked out to the side, only felt it when her foot caught against it and she pitched forward. The ground tried to meet her face, but Kaalinda, still moving on autopilot, reacted like the soldier she was going to be, and rolled instead, tucking her face to her chest and taking the brunt of the force of the fall on her shoulder and back.

Somersaulting back to her feet, Kaalinda felt a final burst of speed catch in her feet, and she surged ahead, ignoring the gasp and stagger of one of her battalion mates still locked in the square of the group.

10

CHAPTER 10

14 DEC 2114

L ATE THAT NIGHT, MOONLIGHT seeped through the dingy windows high on the walls, illuminating the room in twists of pale light and deep shadow. Kaalinda lay awake. To her, the solid gray headboards of the racks resembled headstones. The grinding snore of the recruits deep in slumber sounded like the grating of bone against bone.

She thought of Wilkins. He didn't like her. More than once, she had felt the hate of his glance during inspection, or while working in the compartment. She had heard his whispered comments; cringed at the very idea of being trapped alone with him.

Did he want her dead? He had threatened her with death, but Kaalinda had just brushed it aside, attributing it to anger at her lack of physical ability, or whatever mistake she had just made.

This morning scared her. Had his intent been to kill her? She remembered the kicks and the brutal force behind the steel-toed boots that had slammed into her.

And it had not just been Wilkins. Carter had been there, too, helping him—or at least not stopping him. Other battalion mates had been there, as well, watching. No one had made any attempt to stop the attack, until Ramirez.

She didn't think the others hated her like Wilkins did. But now she knew that they didn't like her, either. She had been slowing them down; pulling down their scores in test after test.

She was a liability to the battalion.

What could she do? She couldn't leave. She didn't have that choice. Not only did the CFoR not give it to her, but Kaalinda refused to allow herself that choice.

The only way, Kaalinda decided, that they would get her out of here without her badge of completion, was in a body bag. To hell with the rest of the battalion. It didn't matter what they wanted from her; all that mattered was what she wanted.

She thought of her dead parents.

Their laughing faces flitted before her closed lids, eyes crinkled at the corners, lips tilted at the ends. She could even hear the tinkling of their voices echo in her ears.

Sorrow washed through her, draining away her anger at their deaths. She should have been there. Would have been there, but she'd been taking school tests.

That's the only reason she was still alive. Everyone in the section had either died during the attack or later in hospital from their injuries.

The CFoR had been her father's idea. He had wanted his sons to be soldiers, to be heroes, to fight and win the battle against the rebels. Neither of his sons had been drafted or had their applications accepted.

But her name had been pulled, so maybe his daughter could.

Kaalinda didn't know why the Aurora Sector, and the prosperous Antietam Farm Belt where her parents had lived, had been bombarded. Most of the community kept away from politics, remaining isolated, and quietly growing food in the long greenhouses for everyone else to eat. It had been safely neutral until then; everyone, on either side of the war, had depended on the food it grew. And those in the farm belt, growing and selling, had never asked many questions from those buying.

What purpose had its destruction served? Were more starving people going to help either side? Kaalinda had never been interested in the war. It had never affected her directly.

Until the attack.

Unlike many of the recruits training, this was nota last choice, a final chance at a future. She had been accepted to school—those tests had been passed with flying colors—to study botany. She had been planning to become a scientist and work on finding new and better ways to grown food.

To follow in her father's footsteps.

And then, she'd received the draft letter. It had been unexpected. She wasn't what anyone would think of as soldier material, but it was like a gift, really. A way for her to find some vengeance.

And the first step was to learn to kill, to understand the mentality of the rebels who had killed her brother and emotionally destroyed her parents with that act.

But how would she make it through to the end of training at this rate? Revenge was a strong motivator, but would it be enough? It was hard enough when you had your battalion mates on your side. Kaalinda was alone in her struggle, and her battalion was siding against her.

Kaalinda stopped thinking about her family and focused on the compartment holding the sleeping battalion. Nasal rasping grated on her ears. The wind whistled a morbid tune through the cracks in the windows high above.

She covered her face with her pillow, trying to drown out the noise around her. She heard her bunk mate, a large Black man who weighed close to two hundred pounds, roll over. The metal springs that supported him groaned under the strain. Kaalinda wondered if they would hold.

It would be a fitting end, Kaalinda thought, to be crushed by a sleeping bunk mate.

She removed the pillow, fluffing it as best she could before stuffing it back under her head.

"Psst!"

Kaalinda stilled in her rack, unsure of the sound.

"MacReady? Are you awake?" The whisper was close, its speaker just on the other side of the iron headboard.

Ramirez.

"What?" Her own voice was raspy, her whisper barely audible.

"Are you okay?"

Kaalinda wasn't sure how to respond to the question. Wasn't sure she even wanted to, so she remained silent.

A long pause. Kaalinda heard the soft breathing, both hers and his. Slowly, their rhythms synchronized.

Tired of waiting for him to give up and leave, Kaalinda whispered, "I guess so."

Kaalinda turned onto her stomach, supporting her body on her elbows, and peered through the bars. All she could see was the back of his head; he was sitting on the floor, back to her rack, resting against it.

"I'm sorry about this morning. I had no idea that was going to happen."

Ramirez made to turn around.

"No!" The urgency in her voice made him stop. He sank back.

Kaalinda didn't want Ramirez to see her. The tears were too close to the surface. She needed to maintain a façade of strength, even to those whom she considered a friend.

When had she started thinking of Ramirez as a friend?

"Do you still hurt much?" Ramirez shifted against the bunk.

"Yeah. I've got some bad bruises and my ribs ache."

"Do you need to go to medical? Does it hurt to move? Your ribs might be broken."

"They don't hurt that bad." Kaalinda lied. No way she was going to medical.

"If you go to medical, they might do something about Wilkins. Take him out of our battalion. Maybe even kick him out altogether."

"They won't kick him out. This is what they train soldiers to do, Ramirez. This is what we'll all be doing when we leave here. If we leave here." The last was almost inaudible.

But Ramirez caught it.

"Don't worry, MacReady. You'll make it out of here. I have no doubt about that."

"Why?" Kaalinda felt sure she would never get out.

"'Cause you've got guts, MacReady. Real guts, not fake bravado like Wilkins." Ramirez' voice was getting lower, slower.

"Real guts?" Kaalinda wondered at that. Bravado? That's not the word she would use to describe Wilkins. "Ramirez?"

Ramirez said nothing. Kaalinda wondered if he had fallen asleep. She wouldn't be surprised. They had spent the entire day struggling through an obstacle course. And once again, the floor of the compartment was strewn with unconscious bodies.

A rasping snort confirmed her suspicions. Kaalinda settled into her pillow, closing her eyes.

She wondered about Ramirez. Why was he sleeping at the end of her bunk? Shouldn't he be in his own rack? Granted, many of their battalion mates were asleep in the middle of the compartment, too tired after the long day to make it to their beds.

Some of them never slept in their racks, sleeping elsewhere to they would not have to make their beds in the morning for inspection.

Kaalinda didn't mind. It didn't take her that long to make hers. Her father had taught her and her brothers how to make military-style beds when they were kids, inspecting their handiwork more harshly that the commanders did now.

Kaalinda sighed. Maybe she should offer to show some of her battalion mates her tricks for making a sharp rack. Maybe some of them wouldn't hate her quite so much if she did.

It was a plan; or the start of one at least. Kaalinda smiled sleepily into her pillow. She would start helping first thing in the morning. She would start with Ramirez. A favor for guarding her tonight.

She had no doubt that was what he was doing. Who would dare finish what Wilkins had started with the temporarily-in-complete-control Master-at-Arms sleeping a foot away?

No one.

Ramirez had proven he could take just about anyone in the battalion. And most of the battalion liked him, or at least respected him.

Kaalinda opened her eyes for a moment, staring at the protruding bulk of the mattress above. She was afraid—afraid that someone else was going to come after her. She hadn't realized it until now.

Knowing she was afraid helped dissipate it. Ramirez was here. No one would dare make a move tonight. And tomorrow night, she would no longer be so sore, she would be better—at least a little better—and she would have other allies inside the battalion. Relaxing, some of her uneasiness slipped away into the shadows, and she followed. She never heard her own sleep sounds meld into those around her.

11

CHAPTER 11

21 DEC 2114

KAALINDA BOUNDED FROM HER rack, grabbing her towel from its hook and her small toiletry bag from the top shelf of her locker. She also grabbed a fresh tee shirt and boxer shorts from the neatly stacked piles on the second shelf.

She was the first recruit to the parallel rows of toilets, the stall doors left open after being cleaned the night before.

Choosing a stall on the end, Kaalinda pulled the door closed behind her, pushing the latch to lock it.

She leaned forward, resting her hot forehead against the coolness of the metal lavatory door. Sweat slid down the damp skin behind her ear. Taking in a deep, relaxing breath, Kaalinda tried to relax the tight muscles of her shoulders and legs.

Yesterday afternoon she had received her second round of hormone shots and her body was reacting.

Kaalinda tried to swallow, but her throat felt dry, like the burnt toast served in the mess hall. The brief thought of food made her stomach flip-flop in her ribcage. Empty, it threatened dry heaves.

She opened her mouth, pulling air into her stomach to calm it. The air worked a little, and

Kaalinda turned to sit on the closed toilet, hanging her head between her knees.

A sudden cold had her shivering. She rubbed her arms with her hands, the goose bumps rough against her palms.

Her shoulders shaking now, Kaalinda stood once again, lifting her knees high, trying to move more blood through her veins.

Flip-flops slapped against cold tile, harsh gasping breaths echoed in the tiny stall.

Kaalinda's stomach overcame her composure and she dove for the toilet, violently flipping the lib back. It cracked hard against the concrete wall, echoing in the quiet.

Vainly, Kaalinda tried to control the spasms that felt like they would tear her in two. Resting her hands against the sides of the toilet, Kaalinda bent her head low.

The toilet smelled of urine and bleach.

The spasms grew worse. Stomach acid splashed into the cold, brown-tinged water of the toilet. Cold drop of liquid hit Kaalinda in the face.

Their coldness felt good.

Kaalinda started at a knock at the cubicle.

"You okay in there?" It was Carter, on watch. "I thought I heard a noise."

Kaalinda swallowed the last of the bile in her mouth. It burned on its return trip to her stomach.

"Hey! Are you okay?" Carter raised his voice.

"I'm okay." The words were whispered into the toilet. Kaalinda didn't have the strength to lift her head.

"What's wrong? Do you need a medic?" Carter wouldn't go away.

Kaalinda stood slowly, leaning against the wall, palms against the concrete to stop her from sliding back to the floor.

"I'll be fine Carter. Just a reaction to the shot I got at medical yesterday."

"Okay." Carter finally walked away. "Call out if you change your mind."

Sniffing, her nose running from the spasms, Kaalinda tested her legs. No longer weak, she stood steady.

Carter was being friendly. Many of her battalionmates were friendlier. Her plan of helping them with their racks had worked. Help them a little, and they will help you back. Kaalinda hadn't thought she had anything to offer her fellow trainees, but had found out that she was wrong.

Helping them had also increased their group scores, and everyone liked that. Bending slowly, she pushed the latch on the side of the tank, then pulled her shorts down, before sinking onto the toilet. She almost fell into the bowl before remembering that the lid was still up. Catching herself, she dropped the lid back into place and sat back down.

Once she had finished on the toilet, she pulled off the tee shirt and shorts she'd slept in and pulled on the fresh ones. The tee shirt pulled at her shoulders and back, straining over newly developing muscles. The boxers were loose at the waist, hanging low on her hips. Kaalinda left her shirt hanging out and gathered yup her towel and toiletry bag.

Quickly, Kaalinda exited the stall, loud spurts from the stall next door warning her that soon the air would be rank.

Kaalinda was not the first to the long row of white porcelain sinks. Ramirez was there ahead of her, shaving. She watched as he lathered his face, then, used a long straight blade to swipe away the facial stubble that had grown since yesterday morning.

"Mornin'." Kaalinda directed the pleasantry into the sink.

"Mornin'." Ramirez returned the greeting.

Letting the water run, Kaalinda applied toothpaste to her toothbrush, adding a little extra to combat the remnants of the morning's purge. The water, slowly losing the orangey-brown hue of rusty pipes, gurgled its way down the drain. Kaalinda vigorously scrubbed the brush over her teeth. In the mirror, she watched the foam drip from the corner of her mouth.

After spitting into the sink, she let her gaze return to the mirror. She barely recognized the face that stared back at her. The face in the mirror was dark brown from the sun, a faint luster of pink on the cheekbones remained from training under the blistering sun yesterday. The cheekbones were prominent in the face, the chin sharp in a strong jaw line. The left cheek was mottled purple and blue, a lingering bruise sustained from Wilkins's attack. It was just starting to turn yellow at the edges.

The whites of the eyes seemed to glow stark in the brown of the face. The hazel of the irises seemed almost green. Dark circles made them appear larger than they were. The hair, minute strands peeking out of the scalp, was slowly growing back. The top of the head was covered with fuzz, the dark red bleached strawberry by the sun.

The lips were dry; small cracks caused by the wind meshing with the cuts from the attack.

No one who had known her before she started military training would ever recognize her now.

She finished her short morning routine and returned to her rack, rehanging her towel and away toiletry bag. The tee shirt and shorts from last night were stuffed into the laundry bag dangling on thehook next to her towel.

She had ironed her uniform the night before, carefully hanging it on the tall post at the end of her rack, near her bunkmate's feet. She pulled the jacket on over her tee shirt, careful of sore muscles not yet recovered.

Her shoulders were tight in the jacket, straining the seams, and the sleeves, rolled according to uniform regulations, were tight above her well-developed biceps. Her pants, once loose and baggy, now fit snugly to muscled thighs and calves, the drawstring at the waist pulled tight.

Kaalinda no longer tried to ignore reveille. It was the key that had released her from the nightmares that haunted her sleep. Each morning she awoke, heart pounding, her body clammy with sweat, images of Wilkins' body embedded on the insides of her lids.

What if he had died? What would have happened to her? And more important, what would Wilkins do to her now? The incident had only fed his hatred of her.

Wilkins had returned to the battalion after a day and a half at medical. Thick white bandages covered his head, concealing the soft fuzz of slowly regrowing hair. He had stared at Kaalinda, not bothering to hide his hatred. Kaalinda had wanted to back into a corner and hide.

Ramirez had watched—silent—from the front of the compartment. When Wilkins had moved towards Kaalinda, Ramirez had restrained him.

Speaking low, only to Wilkins, Ramirez had diverted the situation.

Kaalinda knew it was only temporary though, and that one day, soon, Wilkins would try again. He had decided to hate her, and nothing would change that—not now. The other recruits in her battalion had come to respect her, though. They responded to her comments and helped her as they helped each other.

Ironically, though it hadn't happened instantly, the attack by Wilkins, and her successful defense, had earned her a place on the team.

Kaalinda let her thoughts wander through the possibilities, tying her boots by rote. She wove the leather laces through themetal hooks and eyes, pulling the now pliant leather tight to her calves.

Wilkins would have plenty of opportunity.

Dressed and waiting, Kaalinda watched the others in her battalion get ready for the day ahead, sitting quietly on the floor nextto her rack.

Wilkins glared from the front of the compartment. Standing, arms across his chest, legs wide. He fixed his eyes on Kaalinda.

She stared back, refusing to back down, refusing to show her fear.

Wilkins sneered, his top lip curling high above his yellowed teeth. Crooked, jutting slightly from his mouth, they had the appearance of fangs.

Kaalinda rose slowly, her eyes never leaving Wilkins. She stood quietly, defying the hate pressing against her from acrossthe room.

A line of men, returning from the toilets, broke the contact. Wilkins turned away, speaking to the flag bearer. Kaalinda turned to her rack, making busy by pretending to fix the blankets. On her rack, the sheets and pillow were already neat, the blanket folded and setting on the end. The shelves in her open locker were neat, everything folded per the manual, ready for inspection. She checked over the rack of her bunk mate, tucking in a loose bit, making it tight and even and smooth. She adjusted the pillow and blanket. It looked good.

Kaalinda was ready to start her day.

Though she wasn't so sure she would finish it.

12

CHAPTER 12

21 DEC 2114

"THIS OBSTACLE COURSE IS the first test of your new abilities. We have been training our bodies for a week. Those who do not pass today will go no farther."

Major Denison stood I front of the company, scanning the faces of the 83 recruits watching him. "You will have 30 minutes to reach the end."

Major Denison looked to Captain Carson, nodding at her to continue the instruction.

"You will be broken up by section and run the course with your watch-mates. The BCO, MAA, Guide-on, Yeoman, and Watch Section Leaders will each choose a different section to run with." Captain Carson paced in front of the battalion, her hands clasped tightly behind her back. He didn't let anyone bother

Dark eyes, lined with thick, curling lashes, could curl a recruit into a tiny ball with one, sharp glare. Her hair, short, like her male counterparts, was black and curly.

The chocolate-colored skin on her face was covered with blemishes and scars, and she did nothing to conceal them.

Her uniform fit loosely over her trim form. Her torso was straight, lacking the indent most women had to mark their waist.

Three rows of ribbons decorated her left pocket, including a gold star for valor under fire.

That gold star, centered in the middle of a red and gold ribbon, glinted in the sun. "Any questions?" Captain Carson bellowed the question, the sound echoing against the buildings of the training base.

No one in the battalion moved.

"Very well, then. Fall out and form up."

Kaalinda already stood behind her section leader. Section Two was led by a recruit named Hardison. He was tall, Black and muscular. His voice, however, was soft when he spoke, husky. He made his point with his fist, winning several skirmishes in the barracks, earning his respect with bloodied noses and blackened eyes.

He had a scar on his face, the long, raised line cutting down his right cheek, ending at his neck. He also wore a ring, a plain gold band on his ring finger. He spoke about neither.

No one bothered Hardison. And he didn't let anyone bother those he considered a friend. Kaalinda was happy to be considered a friend.

She was thinking about the scar on Hardison's face, absently listening for a command from one of the battalion leaders, when Wilkins caught her attention. He was watching her, as usual. She had gotten used to that. She didn't like it though. His gaze was like looking into the soul of the grim reaper.

Wilkins moved in her direction. Kaalinda took a deep, sharp breath.

The noisy whoosh of the air expelling from her lungs caught Hardison's attention. "Whassup, MacReady?" Hardison's soft voice drifted gently through the air, slowly invading Kaalinda's stupor.

"Wilkins." The one word was all that was necessary.

Hardison looked up, his sights quickly falling on the form of their advancing battalion leader. Pulling himself to his full height, arms at his sides, he balled his hands into fists.

Wilkins slowed, noticing Kaalinda's protector at the ready. He did not stop though, his steps becoming more deliberate the closer he came.

"BCO Wilkins?"

Wilkins appeared not to have heard the query.

"B-C-O!" The Captain's voice stopped him in his tracks.

He turned toward the voice.

"Did you not hear me?" Captain Carson stood toe-to-toe and nose-to-nose with Wilkins, her words hanging in the air around them.

All movement of the other recruits stopped. Most turned to watch the confrontation, a few tried unsuccessfully to ignore it.

Kaalinda watched from behind Hardison, relief at her momentary reprieve nearly sending her into a swoon. She breathed easily once again.

"Hey." Ramirez' voice, soft, from behind, made her jump.

Turning, she gave him a cross look, then turned back to Wilkins and the Captain.

The tongue-lashing was getting good. Wilkins stood, face flushed red, as Captain Carson gave him a blistering lecture on proper response to an order given by an officer.

Those watching winced as the Captain blasted the BCO. "The next time I speak to you, you will immediately respond, or you will no longer be a part of this battalion. Do you understand me recruit?!"

The masses gasped. Wilkins hated being called recruit. He was the Battalion Commanding Officer and would forcefully remind anyone who forgot.

Kaalinda waited, holding her breath.

Wilkins' hands were clenched tight by his sides and pressing hard against the upper part of his thighs. His face, once red, had paled. His lips formed a tight line over his teeth.

Everyone waited.

"Yes, Ma'am." The words were strangled, barely audible.

"What was that recruit?" The Captain pushed him harder.

Kaalinda wondered if Captain Carson wanted Wilkins to strike at her. The female battalion leader baited her recruits, testing their control of their temper, their reactions. Some had broken, taken a swing, and been cut down by the female officer, and then escorted away, never to be seen or heard again.

"Yes, Ma'am." The words were spoken louder this time, though they were scalded by the heat of anger. Wilkins shifted slightly on his fee, one hand clenching and unclenching at his side.

"That's better." Captain Carson nodded toward Section Four. "You'll run with Section Four. Move it.

Kaalinda hid her smile behind her hand, ostensibly raised to cover a cough. The choking burble sounded convincing.

Ramirez slapped her on the back, hard, right between her shoulder blades.

Hardison turned. "You okay?" Concern made his eyebrows converge over his nose.

Kaalinda nodded, smarting from the tap on the shoulders. She shot Ramirez another glance.

"Looks like I'm running with your group." Ramirez nodded toward Wilkins, sulking next to section four.

"Fine by me." Hardison returned. "I'll probably need help taking care of MacReady." He jerked his head in Kaalinda's direction.

Offended, Kaalinda placed her hands on her hips, mouth open, ready to defend her abilities. Before uttering her first word though, she caught the sparkle of amusement, reflected in both pairs of eyes watching her, and she closed her mouth, reconsidering her comeback.

"Just try to keep up with me, okay?" Kaalinda tried to make the bravado in her voice convincing.

"Yeah, sure." Hardison turned his attention to the rest of the section, silently counting their numbers.

Kaalinda liked having Hardison as a section leader. He looked out for those within his section and treated everyone with equal respect.

Kaalinda stood between Hardison and Ramirez. Sometimes, she felt so much out of her depth at training that she wanted to fail a test. Only her father's memory stopped her.

I will make you proud of me, Papa; you, too Pol. She thought those words now and whispered them to herself every night. It had almost become her prayer, a pledge to her brother's memory, to her father's sorrow.

Right now, she was grateful for their protection, but knew that eventually she would have to face her adversary on her own.

"Section One, get ready." Major Denison barked out the command from the starting line. The group of men that made up that section formed a loose, slightly crooked line along the white paint on the grass.

A red light glowed from the top of a post at the right side of the line. Below it was an unlit green one. The lights were controlled from the observation tower that overlooked the test area.

The observation tower also controlled some of the obstacles in the course. Different scenarios of weather conditions and enemy firepower could be practiced at the touch of a button.

The recruits had no idea what they would encounter on any given day at the test site.

The green light flashed on. Section One entered the course at a run.

The other sections waited at the start at the start of the course. Major Denison and Captain Carson received updates on the section's progress through the course from a small radio receiver. They were given no specifics of the test, merely given the number successfully moving through the obstacles, and the number falling behind.

As recruits passed the finish, they were asked their names by an attendant soldier, who relayed the information to the observation tower, and then to the battalion officers.

After twenty minutes, the number of passing recruits was relayed, as well as the number of failures.

Company 347 lost three recruits.

"Section Two get read!"

Kaalinda stood at the start line, sandwiched between Hardison and Ramirez.

"I don't think I can do this." Kaalinda whispered her confession to no one in particular.

"Sure, you can. You made it through all the practice runs." Ramirez jostled her playfully with his elbow.

"Yeah," Hardison agreed, "You'll do fine."

Kaalinda shook her head. "I have a feeling this is it for me."

Ramirez frowned down at Kaalinda.

"Red…"

Kaalinda's eyes snapped up to Ramirez' face. "Why "Red"?"

Ramirez quirked his lips to one side.

"You have red hair."

"How do you know that?" Hardison leaned forward to look at Ramirez. "Her head's shaved, and what's growing back is bleached blond, just like most of us."

Ramirez glanced at the lights. The yellow was now lit, telling the recruits to prepare. Then, glanced down at Kaalinda.

"I don't need to see the hair on her head to know she's a red head." He paused, eyeing the lights. The yellow went out, and the green illuminated. "I've seen the hair on another part of her body."

Hardison frowned, not comprehending the comment, then, shrugged and entered the course.

Ramirez watched Kaalinda for a moment before entering the course.

As his comment sunk in, Kaalinda felt her humiliation at medical return. A slow burn began to change that humiliation into anger.

Kaalinda started off after Ramirez at a dead run. The only thought in her mind was to catch him, make him admit that he had been the recruit next to her at medical, then beat the bloody crap out of him.

Her anger was fueled by her recent booster shot. Her reaction was immediate and all-consuming. Though she never did catch Ramirez, or give him that beating she thought he deserved, she did pass the test, right along with everyone else in her section.

13

CHAPTER 13

EVENINGS WERE SPENT TRAINING in-house, learning to put your clothing to military standards, to make beds to military standards, to care for the weapons to military standards.

The evening after the obstacle course test was no different. Recruits sat on the floor in small groups, talking low amongst themselves, polishing their boots. The rasp of brushes on boots as the scrubbed the polish into the pits and mars of daily toil, melded with the background whispers.

Kaalinda stood on watch at the door, her hands clasped behind her back, her feet shoulder width apart. The log screen was lit where it sat on the thin podium, the electronic tough pen on his holder.

She listened to the whispers that floated toward her from behind, staring at the flickering screen.

"...naked..."

"...Ramirez..."

" medical "

Only the occasional word was clear, but it was enough for Kaalinda to understand the conversations.

They knew.

They all knew. About what had happened at medical, and that she'd been a prisoner at the brig. Probably what almost happened to her at the brig.

Kaalinda took a deep breath, whooshing it back out noisily. Her hands clenched; she gritted her teeth; she couldn't wait for her watch to be over.

The small clock in the upper left screen of the log began to blink. She had ten minutes left until she was relieved.

Kaalinda touched the screen, scrolling through her log entries, checking them before she had to give a pass-down. Everything was in order.

"Hey! Your relief is here." Smith stood at her left elbow, glancing over her shoulder at the log.

"Hey! Thanks for being early. Nothing major to pass on. Things are quiet. Last round was a half-hour ago. All was secure."

Smith nodded.

Kaalinda signed her name, then, handed the pen to Smith, who signed just to the right of Kaalinda's signature.

Turning to face each other, they quickly saluted. Smith took his place behind the podium. Kaalinda walked back to the racks. Conversations halted as she passed, only to start once she was safely by.

Sitting down at the end of her rack, Kaalinda propped the ancient rifle across her knees. It was only used for show, no ammunition was made for it anymore, but the recruits still had to take it apart and perform maintenance them once a week.

Kaalinda placed a single drop of lubricant on the trigger, working it into the mechanism. Once it was moving smoothly—without a sound—she began to polish the wooden handle.

She was still rubbing it with an old t-shirt when Ramirez walked by. She could tell it was him without looking up—her fellow recruits sitting nearby had quit their low whispers.

Humiliation and anger swelled once more in Kaalinda, and, without considering the consequences, she shot her foot out a few extra inches.

Unsuspecting, Ramirez walked right into her outstretched toes, and landed, face first, on the tiles in front of her.

Kaalinda didn't bother to look up, but continued to vigorously wipe at her weapon, pulling her foot back.

"Fuck." The sentiment was whispered, and followed by a low moan.

"Hey man, you okay?" Hardison spoke, his low voice resonating off the walls. Kaalinda could just see his hand reaching down to help Ramirez to his feet.

Ramirez grasped Hardison's hand, pulling himself to his feet. Gasping, he placed on hand to his stomach, bending over, and breathing deep to restore his normal breathing. "I just got the wind knocked out of me."

"MacReady." Hardison spoke again, "I want to see you in the gear locker, now!"

Kaalinda jumped to her feet, carefully setting her weapon on the floor. She ignored the covert glances of her battalion mates and stalked to the small closet that contained the cleaning supplies.

Whispers grew as she passed.

Kaalinda understood why. Punishment was meted out in the gear locker. Usually the recruit would exit with a bloody nose and several bruises.

This would be the first time Kaalinda had been to gear locker.

The door hinges creaked, the ominous sound only fueling her anger. Hardison would not beat her down. Just because Ramirez was Master-At-Arms, second in command to the BCO, didn't excuse him from retribution.

The closet was dark, and smelled of bleach and wax, remnants of both pooled on the floor. Shelves of various cans and jars covered one wall. The flat surfaces were an inch thick in dust.

Mops and brooms were propped haphazardly in a lopsided rack. Lumps of dust balled into the black bristles of the push broom. The once white mop heads were stained a dingy gray, and emitted a sour, musty odor.

The gear locker was the one place that was not inspected.

Kaalinda flipped the light switch next to the door, only one of the four strips responding to shed its dim illumination through the small room.

She crossed her arms and leaned against the wall next to the mops and brooms, scuffing the toe of her right boot through the pile of dirt left from the last hasty cleaning spree.

Pushing her bottom lip out, she kicked a rusty metal bucket resting next to the mops. Its clang echoed in the small space.

It didn't make Kaalinda feel any better.

The door opened, momentarily filling the room with light from the hall, then quickly closed.

Kaalinda continued to stare at the floor.

A pair of black boots moved into her line of vision, the toes slightly scuffed by dust. Those boots did not belong to Hardison; they weren't large enough.

"MacReady..." It was Ramirez.

"Don't say a word." Kaalinda jerked to a rigid stance, hands balled into tight fists at her sides. "Why didn't you tell me earlier that you were the one with me in medical that first day?"

"I figured you would be embarrassed, so I thought I would keep it to myself." Ramirez leaned back against the door, quickly checking to make sure it was closed and clasped before setting his whole weight onto it.

"So, you thought you would bring it up in front of half the battalion?" Kaalinda screamed.

"They can all hear you." Ramirez watched her from behind half-closed eyes, his voice low and calm.

"At this point, I don't care. The all pretty much know the truth, or else have come up with an even more embarrassing story."

"I'm sorry about that; I just thought you could use the extra motivation to get through the obstacle course."

"I didn't need any extra help getting through the obstacle course."

"Could have fooled me. I thought you were going to lose your breakfast before you even started." Ramirez shifted slightly, placing his weight on his other foot, crossing his arms.

Kaalinda stopped. Her hands hung at her side. Ajar of some unlabeled, amber liquid sat on the shelf nearby. Without thinking, Kaalinda grabbed the jar and threw it at Ramirez.

He ducked.

The jar exploded against the door, its contents splattering across the floor. The odor of an astringent spread through the musty air in the closet.

"Look, Macready, you're going to have to learn to control that temper." Ramirez pointed a long finger at her.

Kaalinda picked up a bucket—it still contained the last of the water used to mop the floor—and pitched it in his direction.

The water sprayed as the bucket moved through the air, landing on the floor and on Ramirez

Ramirez stared for a moment at his now damp uniform, then picked up an open can of wax, and launched his own attack.

The wax hit Kaalinda on the chest, momentarily stunning her. The wax was cold, and thick, sliding beneath her belt to run down her leg.

Kaalinda lunged at Ramirez, pushing him back against the door.

The door cracked, the hinges straining to keep it in place.

She felt the warm whoosh of air against her cheek, Ramirez' breath exploded from his lungs. His fingers bit into her waist, pushing her away.

Changing strategy, Kaalinda began to punch, then, kick.

Ramirez wrapped his arms around her, obstructing her movement.

"Arr...." Kaalinda growled, struggling in his grasp.

"Red, Red..." Ramirez voice crooned into her ear. He rocked side to side, taking Kaalinda with him.

"Mmmm..." Kaalinda moaned and stopped fighting, sagging in his arms.

"It's okay, Red. Everything's going to be okay." One hand moved up to Kaalinda's head, awkwardly stroking her nearly bald crown.

That's when the tears started. Slow at first, then picking up speed, they fell from her eyes, rolled down her cheeks, before falling from her chin.

Ramirez held her, gently rocking, holding.

"Everything will not be okay."

Her words were spoken faintly; Ramirez barely heard them. He leaned closer to her, placing his ear next to her mouth.

"Why?" He whispered to question.

"He's dead. Killed. My parents...are not the same anymore. He'd be so proud of me. Dad...he doesn't even know I'm here."

Her words were interspersed with sobs, and the occasional hiccup.

Ramirez gently patted her back. "Who's dead? How did they die?"

"My brother, Pol." Kaalinda moved her hands to her face, wiping her nose on the back of her hand. "He was a soldier. In the 7th Protectorate Brigade. He died in the attack on the Aurora Farming Belt. He'd volunteered for that Brigade to since that's where we lived."

Ramirez stiffened.

Kaalinda felt the change, pushing away to look up into his face. In the shadows, she couldn't discern his features, his mood.

"What's wrong?"

"Nothing. I'm just surprised that you're from there. I would have thought that would have disqualified you from service. The radiation, and all."

Kaalinda frowned. "Radiation? Individual exposure is limited and a lot of the farming is done under pod covers. Sometimes the direct sun is too much for the plants." She moved away from Ramirez, reaching out for balance when her foot stepped in a pool of wax, sliding out and back.

Regaining her balance, she removed her hands from Ramirez' chest, wiping her palms down her pants.

"Sorry about tripping you. I'm not sure why I got so angry." Kaalinda looked at the floor, swirling the dust into the pooling wax with one toe.

"S'okay. I think you just needed an outlet. Feel better?"

Kaalinda nodded.

"Let's get out of here, eh?" Ramirez turned to open the door, the hinges sticking momentarily, before swinging wide.

Kaalinda narrowed her eyes when the bright light from the hall hit her. She shaded her eyes, letting them adjust, before following Ramirez.

14

— • —

CHAPTER 14

24 DEC 2114

KAALINDA HEARD THE SHARP click of the automated metal clasp at the same instant she felt them close over her feet. A hard knot of fear tightened in her stomach. Closing her eyes briefly, she took a deep breath, exhaling it with a loud whoosh. She heard the noise repeated a dozen times around her.

Along with eleven battalion-mates, Kaalinda was about to be locked in the gas chamber, a round steel tank 20 feet across, and 20 feet high. In the wall of the metal hull facing north, an airtight door stood open, allowing the instructor to leave after relaying his last instructions to the recruits.

Three hatches in the ceiling were closed, sealed from the gray-green sky and orange tinged clouds outside. Rope ladders led up, anchored to the floor by metal hooks.

"You have 30 seconds to orient yourselves to your surroundings. Then the door will close, and the gas will fill the chamber. After another 15 seconds, you will feel the clasps release. At that time, it is your mission to get out of here." The instructor walked from recruit to recruit, checking that the clasps holding their feet were tight, with nothing obscuring their movement.

"If you are not out within five minutes, the door opens, your battalion-mates retrieve you, and you fail."

The instructor stood, stretching his back slightly as he did, then, adjusted his belt and trousers.

"Any questions? Good." He left through the still open door, closing it behind him with a final clang.

Darkness descended like a smothering blanket, encompassing the recruits with its totality.

A soft hissing signaled the beginning of the test.

Kaalinda couldn't see the powdery gas rush out through the spigots in the floor, but she could feel it begin to wrap around her legs as it rose through the air.

She felt its coolness slide through the material of her pant leg, its powdery itch beginning to chaff against the skin of her leg. Like slinky talons of death, it crept upwards, inching its way to her face.

Reflexively, Kaalinda arched her head back, raising her nose as high as she could. She closed her eyes, hoping her eyelids would protect her eyes from the gas.

Rising through the warm, thinning air in the tank, it soon reached her face. Reflexively, Kaalinda took a deep acrid breath of sulfur, rough like sandpaper on the inside of her nose. She gasped, opening her mouth wide; the gas was dry fire to her tongue and mouth, searing the moisture from their surfaces.

Instinctively, she tried to take in more air, but only more choking gas was available. She gathered what was left of the saliva in her mouth, and spit. It didn't help.

Kaalinda could hear the rasping, choking breaths of her fellow recruits as they vainly tried to breathe. Their coughs echoed in the confines of the tank. The powdery gas filled their lungs, and their lungs desperately tried to expel the offensive vapor. The gas permeated her eyelids. Her eyes burned hotly, watering heavily in a vain attempt to clear away the intruding vapor.

The clasps on her feet released with a deep click, freeing her feet. She felt the shadowy figures of the other 12 recruits lurch forward, arms stretching out in search of a ladder to escape. Their panic was like part of the gas surrounding them.

Kaalinda dropped to her knees. The air was clearer here, the powdery gas rising up. She breathed more easily, taking in long drags of heavy air.

The faint caress of warmer air brushed against her cheek. Slowly, she crawled in the direction from which it came.

Frantic recruits rushed around the tank, reckless now in their attempts to find the way out. They bumped into each other, knocking each other down. Chaos ruled.

Kaalinda found the spigot, the noxious fumes spurting into her face. Her eyes burned even more as it fed straight into the delicate orbs. Tears ran down her face, dripping onto the floor, leaving behind wet tracks of relief on her cheeks.

Fumbling in the dark, she felt around with her left hand, searching for the ladder she knew was close by.

She found it almost immediately, and stood, readying herself for the climb out. Her right foot was perched lightly on the first rung when a distressed cry stopped her.

She knew the eleven recruits in the tank with her. She knew their names, where they came from, why they joined the military. The were her battalion-mates, comrades, and perhaps even friends.

She couldn't leave them behind.

Stooping, she unlaced her left boot and pulled it off, placing it over the spigot. "Follow my voice," she croaked, her throat closing tightly around the words, the powdery gas making speech difficult, "I have a ladder." She tried to yell, but it didn't work.

The first recruit to respond ran straight into her. She quickly grabbed his grasping hands, placing them on the side ropes of the ladder. She reached up, grabbed his face, and pulled it down next to hers.

"When you get up there, try to open the other hatches to let some light in, and the gas out." Speaking hoarsely, she directed the words straight into his ear.

She felt, rather than saw, the recruit nod, then, felt the jerks of the ladder ropes as he began his climb up.

The second recruit hit her in the back, pushing her into the ropes. Quickly she steadied the thick strands for the recruit still climbing.

She felt the reassuring strain against her palms as she held the rope. The recruit was still up there.

"Sorry." He mumbled, coughing right into Kaalinda's face.

Remaining silent, Kaalinda put his hands on the ladder as well.

"Stay at the top, help the others, and call out who's made it out."

He had just started his climb, when the first recruit pushed open the hatch, and light flooded the tank.

Rays of gold shot into the dark, illuminating the wisps of green filling the tank. The wisps spiraled upward, seeking release as much as the recruits did.

Kaalinda looked up, saw the first recruit pulling himself out and looked around, squinting in the hard, misty air.

She was surrounded by green smoke. Plumes of the gas continued to waft upward to the opening above, like gauzy banners along the parade route.

With the addition of light, the other recruits moved toward the ladder, pushing at each other to get out first. Kaalinda let them battle it out and moved to find the next ladder.

A recruit had already found the ladder and was half-way up. Kaalinda tried to locate the others left in the tank, looking to her left and right. The ladders were filled with scrambling arms and legs.

The third hatch was opened from above, the light from it falling on the prone figure of a recruit.

"MacReady!" A call from above drew Kaalinda's attention, drawing her gaze up. She raised her right hand to shield her eyes from the glare of the sun, squinting to make out the figure calling down to her through the hatch. "It's just you and Tucker left!"

Kaalinda didn't vocalize her answer, instead, she gave a "thumb's up", letting the figure know the message was understood.

Looking around the now empty tank, she found Tucker, sprawled on the ground, his face turned to one side, his left hand protectively cupped over his mouth and nose. "Hell!" The whispered expletive hurt her throat, but made her feel better. She was starting to get the hang of swearing.

She moved to the unconscious body of Tucker and dragged him to the bottom of the closest ladder. Her sock clad feet slipped a little on the slick metal floor, made all the worse for the powdery residue left by the gas.

Unbuckling her belt, she tied Tucker's hands together, then, draped his arms around her neck, tucking her right arm through their clasp.

Coughing, Kaalinda grasped the ladder and began to climb. It was easy, until Tucker's feet came off the floor.

His full weight almost pulled her from the ladder.

Gritting her teeth, she held on, the coarse rope biting into her palms. She let loose a grunt, then a groan.

The higher she got, the harder it was to breathe. The gas was trying to escape with her and had concentrated near the openings.

Near the top, Kaalinda could hear the others talking.

"Damn! Tucker's out cold. She's draggin' him out!"

The sudden loss of Tucker's weight caught her off-guard, and she almost tumbled back into the tank.

Strong hands and arms pulled her out with Tucker, and she collapsed on the roof of the tank, dragging huge quantities of fresh air into her lungs.

Someone whacked her hard on the back, trying to help her expel the harmful gas left in her lungs.

Gasping, Kaalinda took command.

"Tucker needs help. Someone work on getting him breathing. Carter, go get medical, let them know we've got a situation."

Her eyes adjusting to the bright light, Kaalinda looked around. They were sitting on the flat roof of the tank, a single ladder extending down to the ground.

"They'll expect us to get him down, I suppose." Kaalinda pushed herself to her feet, wobbling slightly from the effects of the gas. "Three of you get on the ladder, looping one arm around the side rail. We'll have to lower him down."

Kaalinda moved to the prone figure of Tucker, and the recruit bent over him, dutifully blowing air into his lungs. Kaalinda recognized him, it was Smith, from her watch section.

"How is he?"

The recruit paused for only a second. "Nothing yet."

Kaalinda reached out a hand to Tucker's neck, searching for a pulse. It was faint, but steady.

He didn't need CPR yet.

"The guys are ready. Let's get him to the ground quick so medical can help him"

Smith nodded, pausing once again. Together they lifted the unconscious recruit, handing him gently to the first recruit on the ladder. Quickly, but carefully, they lowered Tucker.

Two corpsmen waited at the bottom, oxygen and mask waiting. Tucker wasn't even on the ground when they had the mask over his face and the tanks turned on.

Kaalinda watched from above, worry marring her pale features. Tucker needed to be okay.

With a jerk, Tucker's body convulsed, and his hands ripped the mask from his face. Rolling to the side, he vomited onto the ground.

A corpsman held him steady, supporting his head and neck. The other man turned to the small group of recruits waiting by the tank and smiled.

"He'll be fine."

Kaalinda grinned, giving Smith a high five.

"Wahoo!" Someone from below hollered.

They had all made it through alive, and since they had all gotten out within the time frame, they had all passed.

Even Tucker.

15

CHAPTER 15

24 DEC 2114

"BUT WE ALL MADE it out within the time limit." Kaalinda's patience slipped away, her anger smoldering in the pit of her stomach.

"Recruit Tucker was not conscious." The instructor that squared off against Kaalinda stood tall, arms crossed, palms grasping his biceps. His hair was black, and thick, curling over his forehead. The sides were cut short and neat. Blue eyes bored into Kaalinda, insisting that she backdown.

"You only said we had to get out. You said we would fail if someone had to open the door and drag us out."

Kaalinda was adamant in her argument. Tucker had gotten out in time.

"But he was dragged out." The instructor continued, losing patience. He leaned forward, intimidating Kaalinda with his height and size.

"By his team-mates, through the top. Not by an outsider, not through the door in the side. We worked as a team. We should all pass." Kaalinda stood on tiptoe, pushing her face into the instructor's face. "Once I got out of there, I had no intention of going back in."

The instructor remained silent for a moment.

"You think you should be treated as a team?"

Kaalinda nodded.

"Does the rest of your group feel the same way?" He looked past Kaalinda to the rest of the recruits, standing in a loose formation, waiting for the outcome of the discussion.

Shifting, looking around at each other, the group slowly came to agreement. They all nodded. Lips pulled tight around gritted teeth, Kaalinda nodded.

"Then you all fail!" The instructor pivoted on one heel and marched away.

Dumbfounded Kaalinda stared at the retreating figure.

Smith placed one had on her shoulder.

"Don't worry, MacReady, we're still all with you. Tucker got out of there before the time limit. It shouldn't matter how."

The rest of the group moved to stand behind her, some nodding, others agreeing with a low "Yeah".

Fuming, Kaalinda jerked away from Smith, and kicked at the dry ground. Watching the puffs of dust settle, she fumed. The insides of her boots felt like sandpaper, powder from the gas had caked in them after being placed over the spigots. It was making the skin on her feet burn and itch. The sun was hot, making her sweat. The sweat was mixing with the powder left on her skin, making itching lines of wet track over her whole body.

And the instructor was not only going to fail Tucker—he was now going to fail them all.

"I'm sorry. I shouldn't have pushed so hard." Kaalinda's voice was still hoarse.

It hurt to talk, too.

The medics brought water canteens to them, ordering them to drink. "It will help your bodies expunge the toxins from the gas." He also checked everyone's pulse, and, using a penlight pulled from his pocket, made sure their eyes were dilating properly.

"You all seem fine." He carefully replaced the penlight. "You made it out okay, why so glum? I've never seen a group get out so fast."

"We failed." Kaalinda spoke to the ground.

"Huh?" The medic seemed confused.

"I challenged the instructor that Tucker passed since he got out in time. I asked to be judged as a group." Smith explained, shrugging. "He failed all of us."

Shaking his head, the medic walked back to the one shaded area, a man-made shelter where their equipment was set up. Tucker rested on a cot beneath the shelter, hooked up to a monitor, drinking water from a paper cup.

"At least Tucker's okay." Carter spoke this time. "I don't know how I would have felt if I had passed but he had died or something. Hell, I thought I was going to die until you took over, MacReady."

Kaalinda looked up, glancing from one recruit to another. She was surprised at the respect and gratitude she saw in their gazes.

"He's right." Ramirez walked to the group, having just passed the test himself. "No one co-operated in my group. They had to go in after five of them."

He nodded toward the tank, spewing green gas into the sky. The side door was open, medics and instructors pulling bodies from inside.

They watched in silence. Kaalinda prayed that the recruits would recover, and soon. Who knew what damage the gas had done to them?

Eyes bloodshot, Ramirez turned back to Kaalinda. "You did good, MacReady. You got everyone out."

"Yeah. I got everyone out. Then I got everyone a failing grade."

"What do you mean? How did you fail? You all got out in time."

"The instructor doesn't see it that way. He wanted to fail Tucker. I pushed for him to pass and it backfired. He's failing us all."

Kaalinda turned away from the tank, closing her eyes.

She was scared. She didn't want to admit it, though. One failure and you were gone.

Where would they send her? Where would they send the others? Why couldn't she have kept her mouth shut? She rubbed at her itching forearm, staring at the far skyline of concrete building and dirt-covered bunkers.

The investigators had warned her after the accident with Wilkins to watch herself. Anything could land her in hot water. She could feel them waiting to pounce. She thought she could almost see their shadows in the bare shrubs lining the edge of the nearest building.

"Uh-oh." Ramirez' whisper had Kaalinda turning back to the others.

One of the medics was talking into his radio, the others busily working on a limp camouflaged figure.

Recruits were being pushed away, equipment was dragged from the shelter.

Someone wasn't making it.

"Who is it?" Kaalinda whispered.

"Can't tell." Ramirez strained to see who was still out, leaning to the side to get a better view.

"Oh my God. It's Hardison." Carter's voice cracked.

Kaalinda pushed to the front, desperately seeking out proof that Carter was wrong. It couldn't be Hardison.

"It can't be Hardison." Ramirez' voice echoed her thoughts. "He was right behind me. I was sure he came out right behind me. We found the ladder together."

Ramirez moved forward, too, but stopped abruptly.

The medics put down their equipment, shaking their heads at each other. Whoever it was, he was gone.

The huddle around the figure cleared away. Kaalinda, Ramirez, and the others had a clear view of their fallen comrade before Captain Carson draped a white towel over his face and shoulders.

It was indeed Hardison.

Kaalinda blinked hard, fighting to keep her tears at bay. A soft sob caught in her throat. No one seemed to notice, so she turned away, allowing the tears to flow. What did it matter anyway? She glanced toward the others in her battalion, her eyes falling on the stiff stance of BCO Wilkins.

He was smiling. Not just a half-smile, like maybe his thoughts were just off somewhere else. This was a full-fledged grin, showing his teeth and dimples.

Sickened, Kaalinda felt the red tide rise in her once again. Fixated on Wilkins, she didn't notice Ramirez watching her, or notice when he too began to stare at Wilkins.

"Son of a bitch!" It was his words that drew her attention, the rage draining with the distraction.

Kaalinda turned to Ramirez. "What?"

Ramirez was silent for a moment, staring at Wilkins.

Turning to Kaalinda, he explained. "Wilkins was right behind Hardison. He must have done something to him."

Kaalinda stared at Ramirez, who stared back.

"He's going to make me kill him you know." Kaalinda whispered the words, mindful of the others around them.

Ramirez raised one eyebrow.

She nodded. "He wants to kill me. He hates me. I don't know why, but he does. It's going to come down to him or me one of these days."

Turning back to Hardison, she whispered—more to herself than to Ramirez—"I just hope I'm ready."

At the sight of Hardison, the tears resumed. Wiping at her eyes, unconsciously rubbing more powder into them, Kaalinda stooped to a squat. Hanging her head, she cried silently.

The others, caught up in defying their own grief, ignored her.

She would have been gratified to know hers were not the only wet cheeks in the battalion.

16

CHAPTER 16

28 DEC 2114

LICKING DRY LIPS, KAALINDA gently lifted her suit, careful not to let it snag on the edge of her box. It rippled gently when she touched it. She felt it whisper and glide over her fingers and hands.

It caressed her, inviting her to step into it.

Finding the narrow opening in the side, Kaalinda slowly inserted her left leg, inching it around within the garment, feeling with her toes for the leg opening.

The suit moved, meeting her foot halfway; the leg of the suit gliding up her leg, encasing it in the fluttering fabric.

It was warm.

Kaalinda inserted her right leg, feeling the garment move once again to meet her. It wrapped itself snugly around her contours, slinking slowly up her torso. A tingling started in her lower back, much like the sensations at the machine, but gentle, more like fingers than needles. It moved upward, dancing with every nerve in her back.

Kaalinda had never felt so alive, so whole.

She pushed her arms into the sleeves, basking in the warmth that flowed through her veins. Her body felt like it was encased in liquid life. The slit in the side closed itself, sealing without a seam.

The material stiffened and got heavier, like a shell surrounded her body. Kaalinda moved her arm, expecting to feel resistance to the movement.

There was none. The fabric became almost liquid at the joints as soon as the impulse to move her arm formed, allowing the joint freedom of movement.

Kaalinda ran her hands down her sides, over her hips, and back up to her waist. Where her fingers rushed the fabric, it became pliant, quivering in response to her touch.

Closing her eyes, she felt a dozen fingers gently kneading the muscles of her legs, arms, and torso. She felt almost like she was floating in a warm cocoon, safe and secure. She could imagine the warm silken threads of the cocoon, each separate thread soft and pliant against her skin.

The shell softened and pulsed. It changed to feel more like a heavy skin.

Closing her eyes, Kaalinda could see her blood flowing through her veins, singing as it carried oxygen to her muscles. The muscles convulsed, in rhythm, dancing to the same music.

Kaalinda could hear the strain of the song in her mind. It was hypnotic. Her body seemed to move of its own accord, swaying to the low beat. Her heart kept rhythm. Its beats echoed in her ears. Her lungs moved air in and out, in and out.

She felt at peace.

In her mind she saw a great, silver city, humming with life. People swarmed the ground, weaving amongst each other as they rushed through life. Mothers pushed babies in black carriages down the street, partnered by a slight wind. Businessmen spoke on portable phones and carried hard plastic satchels. Street vendors hawked their wares, ignored by the passers-by. Papers danced in the street, partnered by a slight wind. An automatic sweeper brushed them away, capturing them, sucking them into the bowels of the machine.

Kaalinda watched.

It was a scene she recognized. It might have been any big city in the world today, even some smaller ones. But this one she knew. This one she had visited, walked through its streets with her parents, her older brother.

It was the capital.

The shiny dome flashed in the distance, reflecting the dim sunlight seeping through the dome. The old cathedral tower, long since turned into a museum, cut into the sky, stretching toward the dome.

A red wash of color filled the skies. The dome couldn't filter it out. Everything took on an orange hue.

The wail of a baby filled the air, cutting through what had been a silent picture. People fell, gasping, lips turning blue, skin turning red and then brown and then to ash. Kaalinda could feel their pain, the gasps for air that was no longer available, and the burn of empty lungs. She saw others, apart, separate.

Those people were not gasping. They were breathing. They were watching helplessly as people died right in front of them.

Those breathing were wearing the armor suits—suits that had extended up and around their heads, turning them into dark silhouettes. The gray-green glimmer seemed to jump at her from the distance, reaching for her, pulling her towards them.

She struggled. She didn't want to go. She wanted to stay where she was, where it was warm. She was pulled closer, the air trapping in her lungs, burning hotter.

The smell hit her; hot and sulphury. It burned her nose.

The heat rasped against her skin like sandpaper. Screams rent the air, their shrill timber scratching at Kaalinda's eardrums.

Sobbing, tears falling, Kaalinda gave up the fight. She stopped moving. The smells and sounds receded to dim memories. The vision faded, and Kaalinda drifted for a moment, floating on a warm sea, a gentle breeze wafting through her hair, over her skin, soothing after the heat.

Her breathing slowed, calmed. Clean, cool air moved into her lungs. Kaalinda filled them with oxygen, once more seeing her blood moving through veins and arteries. Her heartbeat in time with the pulsion the life-giving liquid.

Darkness fell before her eyes, lightening to gray, then white. But it was not bright. It was misty, like fog or clouds. A dark blot appeared in the distance, getting larger as it came closer. It began to take shape, find form.

A face loomed before her, elongated, gray. Dark green eyes in deep sockets stared into her. Kaalinda stared back in wonder. It was not human, but something more.

"Only you hear our message. You must make the others hear. It is your duty." The voice had an accent Kaalinda couldn't place, the words slurred and singsong. The face contorted, stretched, turning into the face of her brother, Pol. "It is your duty." He repeated, his voice changing to the one her father used when giving her a reprimand. "It is your duty..." The last word stretched out, echoing.

It faded away, shifting to smoke that curled upward into nothing.

She was back to floating. She felt uplifted; it was almost spiritual.

17

CHAPTER 17

24 DEC 2114

TUCKER STOOD AT THE edge of the shelter, an odd look on his pale features. Kaalinda moved slowly toward him, not wanting to startle him, he was seemingly entranced by the white-shrouded form of Hardison.

"Tucker?" Kaalinda spoke carefully, from just behind his right shoulder.

Tucker turned at her voice, but didn't seem to see her, gazing out in a stupor.

"Tucker?" Kaalinda raised her voice slightly, trying to draw his attention.

Slowly, Tucker lowered his gaze, staring a moment at Kaalinda before speaking. "That could have been me." The words were whispered so low, Kaalinda barely heard them. She did understand the reason for his stupor though.

"If you hadn't been in there with me..." Tucker let the words trail off, turning back to the solitary figure lying on the yellowed grass next to the tank.

The next group was still waiting to enter the tank, standing aloof to the side, trying to look nonchalant. They spoke lowly to each other, looking anywhere but at Hardison.

Captain Carson and Major Denison were speaking to the instructor, standing apart from the groups of recruits waiting to complete their training.

Ramirez joined Kaalinda and Tucker beneath the shelter, stretching one arm up to lean against a support, the other hand tucked into his pants pocket.

"Doesn't seem right, does it?" The words were spoken to Kaalinda, Tucker once again lost in his own thoughts.

"It would have solved a lot of problems if it had been Wilkins." Kaalinda knew she could speak the treasonous words to Ramirez without fear. After all, he knew fully what Wilkins was capable of.

"That is true."

"Why Hardison? I thought he would have done something to me again."

"He did. Hardison always tried to help you—he looked after everyone when he could. You don't have him anymore." Ramirez shifted position, crossing his arms, leaning his back against the support. "He and Hardison clashed several times over the way he treated you and some of the others in his section."

Kaalinda thought a moment, scuffing her boot through the fine layer of sand on the concrete floor of the shelter, absently drawing an "H".

"So, this is my fault."

"No. I think Wilkins would use any excuse to do something like this." Ramirez watched Kaalinda from beneath hooded eyes. "That's why he's so good at it."

Kaalinda jumped when Tucker spoke. Ramirez moved away from the support. Neither had realized Tucker had been listening to their conversation.

"Few of us in the battalion have stood by and let him get at you, not since he attacked you." Tucker's eyes glazed and he stared at a point above Ramirez on the support beam. "None of us are completely safe around him."

Kaalinda looked for Wilkins. He was standing, relaxed, hands in his pants pockets, talking to the Guide-On, Yancey.

They stood, laughing, like nothing untoward had happened.

"Whoa!"

Kaalinda jerked as something struck her. Tucker had collapsed against her and Ramirez lunged forward to catch him.

Grasping his arms, Kaalinda tried to get under Tucker's weight, staggering from the force of it.

Ramirez grabbed him from behind, releasing some of the pressure.

Tucker groaned as tremors wracked his body. Sweat beaded along his brow, and a bit of drool escaped his lax lips.

"Medic!" Ramirez called to the medics still hovering near Hardison's body.

"Let's get him to the cot." Kaalinda nodded to the short, narrow cot Tucker had been resting on earlier.

Ramirez grunted an affirmative response, and then struggled with the awkward weight, stumbling when yet another spasm arched through Tucker.

A medic arrived to help lower him to the cot, one hand pressing against his forehead. "Thanks. I'll take it from here."

Kaalinda and Ramirez moved away, slowly, looking back at Tucker, writhing on the small cot.

"Do you think he'll be okay?" Worry tinged Kaalinda's words. She was feeling guilty again.

Ramirez must have sensed her guilt.

"This isn't your fault, either. Tucker would probably be out there with Hardison if it hadn't been for you."

Kaalinda walked more quickly, leaving Ramirez behind. Right now, she wanted to be alone.

***

"Hey, Red!"

Kaalinda looked up at Ramirez' call, dropping the stick she had been torturing. She was sitting on the dry ground, leaning back against a short, crumbling stone wall, a remnant from when the base was merely open farmland.

The stone was pock-marked and rust-stained, acid rain having eaten away at its surface. The mortar that had originally held the wall together was now dry and dusty, a powder falling to the ground. Small piles of the white stuff littered the ground at the base.

Ramirez' boots crunched on the coarse gravel as he came near, small tendrils of dust winding their way up from each footfall.

He stopped when he towered over Kaalinda, placing his hands on his hips, staring down.

With the sun behind him, Kaalinda couldn't make out his expression. She was in no mood to be left guessing.

"What do you want?" She snapped the words like a whip.

Ramirez took one step back, as if he had been struck. "Hey, I'm not the bearer of bad news."

Kaalinda quirked one eyebrow, then picked up her stick once more, twisting one end through the gravel. "Really?"

"Really."

Kaalinda watched him for a moment. "Well?" She wasn't in the mood to be patient and play games. "Spit it out, I'm busy."

Ramirez laughed. "Busy at what? Sulking? Pouting?"

Kaalinda glared up at him. "I think I have a reason to be pissed. My mouth got everyone in my group a failure, remember? Or has the heat given you amnesia?" Lifting the end of the stick to her other hand, she snapped it in two.

Ramirez raised both eyebrows at that, rearing back slightly, putting his left hand to the ground for balance. "Well, actually...you didn't get them a failure. You just have to do it again, and you all have to get out."

Kaalinda dropped the stick, her mouth fixed in a small "o".

"Really." Ramirez answered the unspoken question.

"When?"

"Right now." Ramirez stood, extending one hand to help Kaalinda to her feet.

Once standing, Kaalinda brushed the dirt from her backside, warily watching Ramirez. "You're not joking with me, are you?"

"No way. I want to remain in one piece. I saw what you did to that stick." He began to walk back to the trainer, jerking his head back, referring to the stick she had broken.

"Why?"

Ramirez scuffed one foot, looking down, then away before answering. "Hardison."

Kaalinda stopped. Her loud gasp stopping Ramirez, too. He turned to look at her.

"I think they decided that their harsh treatment of your group may have been partially responsible for Hardison's death. No one was willing to help him get out for fear of failing themselves."

"But, Wilkins..."

"None of them saw him. They weren't inside to know that Hardison was right behind me. No one asked me anything."

Kaalinda nodded, staring into the hazy green horizon. "It's going to rain."

Ramirez turned his gaze to the horizon as well. "Yup. Kinda looks like it."

"What about Tucker? Does he go in with us?" Kaalinda turned the conversation back to the matter at hand.

Ramirez shook his head. "Medics won't let him. He'll have to make up a different day, with a different battalion."

"That'll be hard. He won't know anyone. Won't trust them."

"They won't know him, either. Just that he needs to take it again. Odds aren't good that he'll pass." Ramirez began moving again, trailing his right toe in the dirt, making a long shallow furrow.

Kaalinda stared a moment longer, then nodded, quick and sharp. "Let's go and get this over with. I want to get done in time to make chow."

She passed Ramirez, taking the lead back to the rest of the battalion.

18

CHAPTER 18

28 DEC 2114

"**Y**OUR ARMOR IS READY."

Captain Carson's announcement caused the hushed voices of the battalion to pause.

They had all heard of the special 'armor' the military used. Some had even seen it in action, preventing the wearer from harm from laser and projectile weapons, a flash of blue energy the only hint that something was there when the soldier was hit.

Kaalinda had never seen the armor, only heard the amazing stories of the other recruits, seen the flashy ads at school pep rallies. Her stomach trembled, the small quivers threatening to send her breakfast hurling upward.

Her stomach was forever acting up on her now. She'd had three injections, each one making her nauseated, weak, and tired the night after it was given to her.

She was starting to get used to it though. She knew to spend those nights near the toilets with her blanket to ward off the cold chills, and a cool, wet cloth to help make the hot flashes more bearable.

However, in the moments like now, when excitement caused her body to react, the nausea came back; sometimes she could not control it, and would run for the nearest toilet, retching.

But this was not one of those times. The little wiggles in her stomach were not that bad.

At the front of the room, Captain Carson and Major Denison stood side-by-side. The BCO and MAA stood at attention next to their racks the same as the rest of the battalion.

"This armor is specifically designed for the individual recruit," Captain Carson projected her voice over the excited hum of the battalion.

Each recruit stood at the head of their rack, staring in excited awe at the black boxes neatly lined up in two rows down the center of the room. Each box was engraved with a service number on a small brass plate at one end. A shiny brass handle was attached just above the plate.

Kaalinda noted that her box was slightly smaller than the others; it made sense, since she was a good head shorter than everyone else. The injections had helped her get stronger, but, just as she had assumed, they had done nothing to make her taller.

But her box was more of an oval, instead of a sharp rectangle, and the color shifted from blue to green if she tilted her head. No one else seemed to notice; they were too enthralled by what was waiting in their own boxes.

"There is a microchip in the head gear, specially programmed to work with the one implanted in your neck when you arrived. In this way, it not only monitors your bodily functions, but it can communicate them to you, as well."

Captain Carson paced slowly down the length of the room, weaving among the boxes, looking at the boxes rather than the recruits.

"It can monitor heart rate, body temperature, hunger, and fatigue. Depending on the strength of the connection, it may monitor other functions." Captain Carson stopped walking. "The armor itself is semi-organic in nature, molding itself to your body. It is designed to accommodate fluctuations up to 10 percent."

Captain Carson rotated in her spot, staring at each recruit for a moment, before moving her eyes to the next. Once she had made eye contact with everyone, she spoke again.

"In no instance, for any reason, will you put on another recruit's armor. There is enough discrepancy between individuals that your brain could be severely damaged by the process." Captain glanced around the room again. "Is that understood?"

"Yes, Ma'am!" The entire battalion answered as one, the sound reverberating from the walls.

"Good." Captain nodded. "Open your boxes."

The boxes were locked. A small touch pad was located near the handle. Kaalinda placed the thumb pad of her left hand on the small, blue-green square. It was cold, but soon grew warm as the mechanism processed its function.

The box top popped up two inches.

Kaalinda lifted the top, extending the concealed hinges as far as they would go. Swallowing hard, she looked over the contents.

Inside, on a black, contoured pad rested a gray-green suit. The elliptical-shaped helmet lay tucked at one end, touching the fabric at the high neckline of the suit. At the opposite end of the box, were the special boots and the reinforced pads she could opt to wear at her shoulders, knees, and elbows when the terrain or mission warranted.

Kaalinda reached out her right hand, touching the sleek-looking garment with her fingers.

It quivered. The movement rippled across its surface, like the waves made by a pebble dropped into a bucket of water.

She withdrew her hand quickly, glancing to her left to see if Captain noticed.

"It's okay to touch it, MacReady. It's yours. In fact," Captain turned in a semi-circle, addressing the entire battalion, "I want you to put them on."

"Wahoo!" Carter was enthusiastic, snatching the suit from his box. It wiggled and jerked in this clasp.

"Not so fast there, Carter." Captain strode toward him, one hand outstretched to stop his movements. "It's not that simple."

Having stopped Carter, Captain turned back to the group. "Remember that strange suit you were fitted for and issued at clothing issue? Its white, looks like a half-metal tank top with bottoms attached."

Everyone nodded.

"You need to put that on first. The back is reinforced with an alloy metal, making the initial contact with the suit superficial. There is no guarantee that the suit is without defects. It can be dangerous to put a suit on for the first time without some sort of protection."

The battalion turned to their lockers as if one body, opening the locks and pulling the small white garment out.

"This needs to be put on directly over your skin." Captain looked directly at Kaalinda. "MacReady, you go change in the head. I'll call for you when the others are dressed."

Kaalinda nodded, using quick strides to stride to the toilets.

She was glad Captain was in charge of this activity. Major Denison would have just told them all to change, then rebuffed her if she had made any move to leave. She thought he took the "equality of recruit" code a little too far.

Relieved that she would not have to bare herself in front of her battalion mates, nor see them bare skinned, Kaalinda quickly changed into the one-piece suit.

The white fabric was soft and flexible, except for a shiny, grayish strip. The stiff strip fitted neatly to her back, snuggling up close to her spine and extending up her neck to where her hairline. The top did look like a tank top, the bottom like attached, slim-fitting shorts. The fabric was light weight, revealing the structure of her skin and muscles underneath.

Staring at herself in the mirror, she was embarrassed to find her nipples evident beneath the fabric, her high breasts clearly defined.

Turning, she found the suit to fit the same in the back, the cheeks of her bottom separated at the top by the rounded point of the lead strip. The seam of the suit cut between the cheeks of her buttocks, outlining them beneath the thin cotton-like fabric.

Kaalinda could feel a thin veil of color fill her face. She would not be entirely spared of embarrassment today; she would rather have just stripped down naked in front of the others and put the suit on without this meager protection.

"MacReady!" Major Denison called from the doorway.

"Coming, Sir." Kaalinda's voice was hoarse. Taking a deep breath, she left the toilets and walked into the main room.

Head held high, she walked quietly between the two rows of recruits, her bare feet silent on the cold floor.

Goosebumps covered the flesh of her arms and legs, and only made her nipples all the more prominent.

She glanced neither to the left nor right, but stared straight ahead.

Finding her place in line, she stood at attention, feeling the color once again rise up her neck to her face.

No one in the room spoke. All that was heard was the rough breathing of everyone in the room.

Once in her place, Kaalinda could no longer avoid looking at another recruit. Carter stood across from her. Kaalinda tried to look him in the eyes but found his eyes intent elsewhere on her person.

Giving up on eye contact, Kaalinda decided to let her own eyes rove. She let them lower over Carter, noting the blond curls that peeked out of his armpits, and the way the fabric clung to his torso. Allowing her eyes to drop downward, she wasn't ready for the protruding member between his legs.

Carter was most definitely aroused.

Kaalinda darted her eyes upward once more, staring at a spot on the black smudged wall just above Carter's left shoulder.

Licking suddenly dry lips, Kaalinda slowly recovered her composure.

Was Ramirez in the same state?

She wasn't quite sure why the question popped into her head. She just knew that once it was there, she had an uncontrollable urge to find out the answer.

Without losing her straight posture, Kaalinda tried to look to her right. She couldn't see him. Standing to the far right, at the front of the room, Ramirez was completely concealed from Kaalinda's view.

Cursing her fate at being assigned a rack on the wrong side of the room, Kaalinda forgot all about the other recruits and their stares.

She wanted to get into her suit though. She moved her eyes to look at the battalion leaders quietly talking to each other at the front of the room.

Since the rest of the room was unearthly silent, Kaalinda could make out bits of pieces of the conversation.

"I told you she should have put the suit on in the toilets." Captain was obviously miffed.

Kaalinda couldn't hear the Major's reply, but it made Captain even angrier. She turned her back on Major Denison and spoke to the recruits.

"Put your suits on!"

Kaalinda dove for her box, reverently stroking the suit inside, before carefully pulling it out.

"Be careful. Let the suit adjust this first time. Put one leg in and stop before the other. We want to make sure everything is functioning as it should." Captain continued to issue warnings, even as Carter pulled his suit entirely on in one swift movement.

He staggered on his feet, his face turning white beneath his deep tan. The suit turned a mottled gray-black, and quivered around his body, a hole appeared over the middle of his chest, then closed up again.

Carter jerked, the suit rippling violently, like storm waves thrashing against a beach. He fell to the floor, writhing in the once-again gray-green suit.

"Open it up!" Captain issued the order, even as she ran to do the deed herself.

Kaalinda dropped her own suit, darting across the room to help Carter.

He had stopped writhing, and lay unmoving, staring up at the dusty ceiling.

"Carter?" Kaalinda placed one hand gently on his shoulder.

Captain peered over her shoulder, worry etching her already tight features.

"Wow!" Carter's voice was shaky, but strong. "Will it always be like this?"

"No." Captain straightened, placing her hands on her slim hips. "You're lucky, Carter. I've seen people get torn apart when the rushed their suits the first time."

Kaalinda stood, moving back to her own suit left draped over the edge of the black box.

"Carter, you get double watches for a week." Captain marched back to the front of the room after giving the command, disgust hanging from her face. "Watch leaders, he gets MacReady's watches. Since she was first to help him, she gets the benefit of his folly."

Turning back to the dumbfounded group, she nodded. "You may continue. Just remember to go slow. Anything starts to feel wrong, stop."

19

CHAPTER 19

28 DEC 2114

"IT'S ALIVE." KAALINDA'S WHISPERED words went unnoticed by the others, too wrapped up in their own first experiences with their "armor."

"MacReady?" Captain walked toward her. "How does it feel?" The older woman was smiling, enjoying the awestruck faces of her cadets.

"It feels..." Kaalinda paused, searching for the right word, but none came to mind. She thought of the message she had been given, but wasn't sure if it had been real or a hallucination. She didn't mention it.

"MacReady?" Captain watched her, worry creeping into her usually austere features.

"Ma'am?" Kaalinda looked up, traces of the effects of the suit still glazing her eyes.

"How did it feel?"

Kaalinda smiled. "Invigorating, Ma'am."

Captain Carson nodded, full understanding mirrored in her brown eyes.

"That would be the energy feedback. You'll get used to it quick enough. Then you'll wonder what you would do without it."

Kaalinda continued to smile, nodding her agreement with the statement. She wasn't sure about not being able to do without the suit, but she was expected to agree with the Captain.

The Captain moved among the recruits, watching their expressions as they experienced the suits for the first time. Noone rushed it after watching Carter.

Kaalinda's thoughts turned inward, to the face that had spoken to her, the voice, the city, the death she had seen.

"Captain?" Kaalinda called hesitantly, unsure of asking the question that now burned in her mind.

The Captain turned and came back to stand before Kaalinda, who now sat cross-legged on the floor.

"Yes, recruit?" The woman clasped her hands behind her back, rocking on her heels.

"Where did the suits come from?" Kaalinda looked up, her hands folded and resting between her crossed legs.

Captain Carson considered a moment before answering, then nodded to herself. "They were originally discovered in a crash site for what we believe to be an alien ship. The suit was examined and tested, and we've been reproducing them ever since."

Kaalinda stared up at the Captain.

Aliens.

She thought of the face she had seen. "What did the aliens look like, do you know?" Kaalinda attempted to sound merely curious.

Captain Carson looked around at the other recruits, most of them were still enthralled by their suits. The others quietly studying their hands or their feet, absorbing the experience.

"They were gray." Captain Carson turned back to Kaalinda. "That is all I know."

Kaalinda nodded.

"Why do you ask?"

Kaalinda thought for a moment, licking her lips slowly to buy time. "I saw something."

Captain squatted in front of her. "What did you see?" She kept her voice quiet.

"A gray face. It spoke to me." Kaalinda leaned forward, placing one hand on the Captain's forearm. "It spoke to me. It said I needed to make you hear the message."

Captain Carson quietly studied Kaalinda's face, then shrugged away her hand and stood up. "Recruits see a lot of things, MacReady—especially the first time they put on their suit. Best forget about it and move on."

Kaalinda watched the Captain move through the other recruits, checking on them. Should she forget? Or should she try to figure out what the hell the message was and try to pass it on?

20

CHAPTER 20

3 JAN 2115

KAALINDA SAT ON THE cold tile, wearing her tee shirt and shorts. Sweat dripped from the short red hair on top of her head. Her wool blanket sat folded at her feet, waiting for the chills. She was currently experiencing a hot flash and had a washcloth cooling in a bowl of cold water. The nausea had settled down; there was nothing left in her stomach to expunge.

A sharp chill swept up her spine. She reached for the blanket, sweeping it around her now-shivering body. She tucked her feet under the hem, burrowing deeply into its folds.

Her teeth began to chatter. Kaalinda tried to hold them still, but it only made her jaw ache.

Leaning her head back against the wall, she closed her eyes, praying for sleep.

The scuffing of combat boots against tile brought her head up. Through blurry eyes, Kaalinda could make out the figure of a fellow recruit, standing above her in a tee shirt, shorts, and unlaced boots.

"Another reaction to your shot?"

Kaalinda recognized Ramirez' voice and nodded her reply, relaxing back against the wall.

"Want some company?"

"Sure." Kaalinda would appreciate anything that might take her mind of how cold she was.

Ramirez sat down beside her, frowning.

"What's wrong?" Kaalinda frowned back.

"The floor's cold." Ramirez stood up. "I'm gonna get my blanket and come right back." He shuffled off again.

Kaalinda's eyes were closed when he returned; she didn't open them. She felt him settle next to her, shifting to get comfortable on the hard tile.

They sat quietly. Kaalinda listened to Ramirez' breathing next to her. The steady in-out whoosh was hypnotic. She felt herself drifting slowly into sleep.

***

Kaalinda awoke to darkness. The light from the emergency lights shed a golden pool of white on the floor near the open door.

She had been drooling.

Wiping the spit from her chin, she accidentally jostling Ramirez, who still sat next to her, gently snoring in his own slumber.

He jumped, startled by the touch. "Wha..."

"Sorry." Kaalinda mumbled, her voice husky from sleep. "I forgot you were there."

Ramirez cleared his throat. "Where are we?"

"In the bathroom. You kept me company, remember?"

Kaalinda felt his nod rather than saw it. "You had another shot."

"Yup."

"Feeling better?" Ramirez' voice was muffled by his hands rubbing over his face.

"Yup."

Kaalinda looked in Ramirez' direction in the dark, wondering what he was thinking. It was cool sitting on the floor; she pulled her blanket closer around her.

Ramirez cleared his throat again, the sound harsh and loud in the darkness.

The beam of a flashlight split the blackness, its end settling first on Kaalinda, then on Ramirez.

"So, you're finally awake. What's up?" It was Carter, on watch once again; he was almost finished with his double-watch punishment.

"Red had another shot today. She had a bad evening. We fell asleep here."

"Hell, I knew you were asleep." Carter turned the light on.

Kaalinda squinted, the sudden brightness momentarily blinding her.

"You okay now?" Carter asked her.

Kaalinda nodded. "Except for the light blinding me, I'm fine."

"Oops, sorry. Didn't think."

"S'okay."

"Want me to leave?" Carter switched off his flashlight and turned to go back to the watch podium.

"Sure." Ramirez spoke, shifting on the floor. "We'll have to leave anyway and get back to our racks."

Carter left with a backhanded wave, his boots thumping on the tile, the noise fading as he moved away.

Kaalinda and Ramirez remained silent for a moment, adjusting to the light.

"You were close to your parents?" Kaalinda had barely noticed Ramirez' lips moving and was surprised by the question. They hadn't really spoken much about things like that since the gear locker.

"Yeah." Kaalinda looked at where her hands were entwined in her blanket. "My dad wanted me to be a farmer, like him, only...maybe an ultra-farmer I guess."

"What do you mean?"

Kaalinda sensed is movement, his head turning, his eyes falling upon her. He rested his elbows on his raised knees.

She shrugged, the blanket slipping slightly on her shoulders. Ramirez pulled it back into position for her.

"Thanks." Kaalinda glanced up quickly, offering a small, fleeting smile before returning her gaze to the lump that was her hands. "He always encouraged me to experiment and not give up or let anyone tell me I was wrong about something without proof. He let me have my own little garden space where I could experiment on plants and test different ways to grown them."

"I still don't understand." Ramirez shook his head at her.

Kaalinda took a deep breath, then pursed her lips, frowning at the cement block wall in front of her.

"He said I could be whatever I wanted. If I hadn't wanted to be a farmer, he would have encouraged that instead. He even let me train with my brother. Pol, who always wanted to be in the military. I didn't want to serve—not then—but he didn't stop me from doing whatever my brothers did. I mean, he knew that a draft was always possible, and he wanted me ready for that just in case, but he never made my life only about that. Even for Pol, he never let that be everything for him."

"Most fathers don't want their children to join the military. Soldiers die." There was an edge to his voice.

Kaalinda glanced at him again, noting his dark scowl. "Everyone dies. Farmers die."

She jostled Ramirez with one shoulder, knocking him slightly off balance.

He pushed back.

"Aren't you proud to be here? Serving your government? Your people?"

Ramirez looked her straight in the eyes, turning her question back on her. "Are you?"

Kaalinda stared back, momentarily at a loss for words. Was she proud to be here? She didn't know anymore. She knew Pol would have been proud of how far she'd made it.

"I should be." Kaalinda whispered back, dropping her gaze, staring at a small fleck of black polish smudged on the tile. "I think I would be if..." Kaalinda let her voice trail off.

"If?"

"I feel like I should be at home, on the farm, with my parents. I'm not. They were so upset when they got the official notice about Pol. I'm all that's left for them. They didn't want me to show up for processing." Kaalinda smiled, ruefully shaking her head."

Another deep, noisy breath. "Anyway, Pol should have finished his two years and then gone to a technical school."

"So—survivor's guilt?"

She shrugged and picked at a piece of lint on her blanket. "Maybe."

Was it?

They didn't speak for a minute, each busy with silent thoughts.

"You know, it's funny. I never expected anyone to attack a farming belt. I mean, we all need food. Even the rebels. They get it from the same farmers everyone else gets it from. There's no way to know, really, if you're selling to a rebel or not. They don't wear big badges that say REBEL."

"They weren't attacked." Ramirez spoke in a rough whisper.

Kaalinda glanced at him.

He had his eyes closed, his head leaning back against the cold cement of the wall. He looked pale beneath his tan, his skin tight across high cheekbones, his chin set and teeth clenched.

"What do you mean? There was video on the news."

"I was there." Ramirez still spoke quietly, keeping his eyes closed.

Kaalinda frowned, pulling the blanket up around her shoulders, hunching forward, pulling her knees to her chest.

"How were you there?" He would have still been young enough to be in school; he wasn't that much older than her.

"I was buying vegetables with my mother. And there was an attack, yes, but not by rebels. It was CFoR."

Kaalinda stared at Ramirez, not quite grasping what he was saying. Then, the whole of it sunk in.

He's been there—and was still alive.

"Why?"

"Why what?"

"Why are you alive? Everyone in the farming belt died."

"Not everyone." Ramirez took a deep breath and stared into her eyes. "Only the folks that worked there."

"But—the video..."

"Doctored. The Government wants everyone to think it was the rebels."

"How do you know it wasn't the rebels?"

He didn't answer.

"Okay, then tell me this: why did they attack? Why would THE GOVERNMENT attack a farming community?" Kaalinda's voice rose, its pitch rising sharply.

"Shh." Ramirez hissed, leaning close.

Kaalinda inched away, forgetting about her blanket. "Are you a rebel?"

Ramirez looked at her, his tongue wetting his lips before he answered. "Yes."

She stood, the blanket falling to the floor in a pool at her feet.

"You killed them." The whispered accusation hung in the air, a think curtain between them.

"I was a kid. I didn't have a weapon. None of us did. I told you it wasn't the rebels that attacked."

She shook her head, breathing harsh, the air hard in her lungs. "It's your fault."

Ramirez didn't respond.

Kaalinda backed away, returning a few steps to retrieve her blanket. Hatred burned through her. Her hands balled into the blanket, twisting the fabric.

Ramirez remained silent, watching.

She turned and left.

21

CHAPTER 21

6 JAN 2115

KAALINDA, TUCKER, AND RAMIREZ held position on a small hill. Hidden in the artificial brush and tropical ferns, they were unseen by the enemy team marching by.

Keeping silent, they watched the line of scuffed black boots pass within inches of their noses.

The boots crunched on the artificial turf, stomping down the plastic tufts of grass. High above, bright lights hung from iron rafters. Rope vines trailed down concrete and plastic posts, adorned to resemble trees.

This jungle was encased within what was once a hangar bay for ancient cargo aircraft. Metal containers now served as rocks and debris.

Once the enemy troops had passed, Tucker signaled that he would follow. Ramirez nodded.

"Be careful." Kaalinda only mouthed the words.

Tucker merely shook his head at her, grinning. Rolling his eyes, he carefully moved forward, remaining silent. He had gotten cocky after his gas chamber retest. He had led a team of strangers out in the second shortest time ever. After that, all his test scores had gotten higher.

Alone, Kaalinda and Ramirez waited.

Shifting her weight onto one arm, Kaalinda reached over to Ramirez, tapping his should with her finger.

Ramirez turned at her touch.

"Why?" Again, Kaalinda only mouthed the words.

Ramirez seemed to understand her question. Rolling to his side, he pulled his small notepad from the large pocket on his thigh, along with the small lead pencil he kept there.

Making as little noise as possible, he wrote his answer on the first empty page.

I DON'T KNOW WHY THE CFOR ATTACKED THE AURORA BELT.

Kaalinda grabbed the pencil and paper. Forcefully, bearing down hard with the pencil, she jotted down her own words.

IT DOESN'T MAKE SENSE.

"The rebels were set up." Ramirez spoke the words aloud, whispering them directly into Kaalinda's face.

"By who?" Kaalinda wiped a hand over his face, removing the droplets.

"I don't know."

"And how did the media and the government get video that shows rebels attacking?"

"How would they get video to begin with? Did you have cameras set up?" Ramirez' nose was only a hair's breadth from her own.

And he'd posed a very good question and she couldn't really answer. "We didn't have cameras. At least...not that I was aware of. No one ever mentioned having cameras."

He stared at her until she dropped her gaze away.

Leaning closer, he kept his lips close to her ear. "I'm beginning to think they're just playing a game with us. All of them. The news people, the government, maybe the rebel leaders. It's just a game to them."

"I don't believe you!" Kaalinda pressed her face so close to Ramirez; this time their noses touched.

They remained in that position, nose to nose, until Kaalinda got a cramp. Breaking eye contact, she rolled to her back, bringing her knee to her chest to relieve the tight knot forming in the back of her thigh. Gritting her teeth, she bit down on the cry of frustration and pain that threatened to burst from her lungs.

Once the cramp had eased, Kaalinda flopped back to the ground, her head thumping against the solid floor beneath the layer of turf.

Ramirez clamped a hand on her shoulder, squeezing.

She jerked, readied her fist for an attack, when she realized that Ramirez' attention was on the bushes on the other side of the clearing.

Kaalinda froze, barely allowing air to enter her lungs.

Someone was coming. Though the noise was not significant, it was discernible in the unnatural quiet of the plastic jungle.

Ramirez moved his hand to his stun laser, his finger loosely circling he trigger. Steadying the barrel against the ground, he aimed in the general direction of the noise.

Kaalinda let out her breath, slow and steady, rolling to her stomach, grasping her own weapon. She tapped Ramirez on the shoulder. Leaning forward, she whispered into his ear. "I'll head around to his back."

Ramirez nodded once.

Inching her way back, she silently dragging her weapon along. Ten feet back, she squatted, looking around for signs of life, listening for sounds of movement.

She heard nothing except the faint whine of the overhead heat lamps.

She moved off.

The plastic leaves of the plastic plants obscured her path. Kaalinda tried to move them away, cringing inside at the rustle she was unable to dampen. In a semi-crouch, she walked, almost duck-like, through the bright green leaves.

She moved in the direction the war-game maps indicated as "south". This was the direction from which the enemy team had marched earlier. Since most of them were now to the "north", she felt it was the safest direction to go.

Sand and gravel marked what was supposed to be a dry stream. Kaalinda paused before emerging from the trees. She peered up then down the stream's path.

She stepped out, freezing the movement instantly when her boot crunched on the gravel. Her stomach knotting, she wondered if there was anyone close enough to hear her.

No one else emerged from the greenery. Exhaling the breath held tight in her lungs, Kaalinda continued, keeping to one edge of the dirt stream, trying to keep her boots on the green turf.

Stopping to check her bearings, Kaalinda pulled the small round compass from the large cargo pocket on her thigh. Giving it a moment to adjust to the artificial electric field, she watched the spinning needle settle. The electric field made the compasses coincide with the directions on their maps.

It was time to turn to the "north", to move behind the noise that had advanced on their position earlier.

Pocketing the compass, Kaalinda checked her weapon, ensuring it was primed and ready to fire.

She listened carefully, interpreting every noise she heard, the distant gurgle of the ancient cooling system pumping water through its rusty pipes, the whir of the fans that provided the artificial breeze, the whine of the electric system that fed the heat lamps.

Wiping a hand across her brow, Kaalinda realized that it was getting hotter. Without their suits, there was no way to regulate their body temperature, unless they started removing clothes.

Kaalinda considered removing her jacket, then tossed the idea aside.

She heard a noise. It was a snap, like a footfall on a branch. It was followed by the slap of plastic fern leaf.

She decided to remove her jacket after all.

Setting her weapon on the ground at her feet, she shrugged out of the garment. Retrieving her weapon, she was in.

Ah, right there.

Taking care, she draped her jacket over a couple of branches sticking out from a concrete tree. Half concealed by leaves, it made the appearance of a person standing in the bushes.

Smiling, Kaalinda looked around for a hiding place. A metal "rock" cluster provided a position elevated above the clearing, giving her a clear view of her quarry.

It was not long before she was rewarded. Wilkins, laser in his hands, shouldered through the trees.

He paused when he noticed the jacket. His smile, showing slightly pointed teeth, made Kaalinda shiver. Lowering his stun laser, he reached his right hand down to his boot, unsheathing a long knife.

Sucking in a startled breath, Kaalinda realized he meant to kill the person he thought was hidden in the trees.

She watched him lick his lips, wipe the remaining spittle from them with the sleeve of his jacket. With his left hand, he reached down, adjusting his trousers, shifting the crotch to the left.

Kaalinda closed her eyes, opening them again when she heard him move. He advanced toward her jacket, knife raised in his right hand, the glinting tip pointed down. His left hand and arm were extended, ready to grasp one shoulder of his prey.

Raising her own weapon—set to stun per the rules—she trained her sight on his torso. She wouldn't have a chance if she missed.

When he paused before the pounce, Kaalinda squeezed the trigger, pressing her body back into the crevasse that shielded her.

The blast of the weapon drove her farther back. Silence reigned when it was over, broken only by the mechanical sounds that provided their artificial jungle.

Breathing hard, she listened, her cheek pressed tight to the metal it rested upon. Hearing nothing, she peeked into the clearing.

Wilkins lay prone on the ground, his face turned toward her. His eyes were closed and his lips were slack so that his mouth was open.

The smell of hot metal and burnt plastic filled the clearing. Kaalinda wrinkled her nose, wondering how the stun laser could simply stun flesh, without damaging the cloth over it, yet would crisp plastic at the merest brush of its beam.

Wilkins' fingers had released their grip on the knife handle, and the blade lay on the ground next to him.

Kaalinda was making to climb down from her perch when another noise reached her ears. Pausing halfway to the ground, she listened, frozen, ready to scramble back to her hiding place.

The noise was rapidly approaching her position, so she pulled back into her secure alcove, peeking from behind a huge, deep green frond.

Ramirez edged into the clearing, followed by Tucker. Both had their weapons raised in front of them, Tucker watching their backs. Ramirez tripped over the stun laser Wilkins had discarded in favor of his illegal knife. Tucker bumped into him as he kept his head turned to the rear.

"What the...?"

Kaalinda heard the whispered words and crawled from her lair. "He was going to kill me." As soon as her feet touched the ground, she reached around for her weapon.

The words caused Ramirez to jerk his head back and raise his weapon. Tucker spun around to face Kaalinda, his eyes falling on the decoy jacket, then to the unconscious Wilkins.

"What happened?" Tucker asked.

"He pulled a knife."

Ramirez walked over to Wilkins, jabbing the knife with the toe of his boot.

"But that's illegal." Tucker still stood on the edge of the clearing, looking at Kaalinda.

Kaalinda shrugged. "He didn't seem to care."

Ramirez squatted down next to Wilkins. He examined the pale powder left on Wilkins jacket by the laser blast. "Good shot, Red."

"Thanks." Kaalinda crossed the clearing, pushed Tucker out of the way, and stood where Wilkins had stood upon seeing the jacket.

Staring at the still partly concealed jacket, coldness fell over her, goose bumps spreading over her flesh.

In plain view, turned up by a ridge branch, was the small green band beneath the hem that clearly read MACREADY in black ink.

22

CHAPTER 22

7 JAN 2115

"Yesterday, you battled each other as teams. Today, you will battle each other as individuals." Major Denison spoke to his battalion of recruits that stood in formation beside the pit. "You will continue to train and test without your suits. You must pass this training before moving to the next phase. There, you will learn the intricacies of the suit. Any questions?"

No one raised a hand.

"Let's begin. Form two lines, one at each ladder into the pit. Fall out!"

The recruits broke rank, splitting neatly down the middle. Two straight lines formed on each side of the concrete pit.

Kaalinda was third from the front, waiting in line for her turn at hand-to-hand combat. She was on the side of the pit led by Captain Carson and Ramirez; Wilkins was on the other side with the major. The combat test would take place in a concrete pit, 50 feet square and 15 feet deep. A ladder descended on each side to provide access for the combatants.

Kaalinda could not see the current fighting, but she could hear it. The growls and grunts, moans and groans told the story. And from the wide grin on Major Denison's face, his side was winning.

The noises stopped.

The head, then the shoulders and torso of one recruit appeared at the top of the ladder on the opposite side of the pit. When the recruit was completely out, he raised his hands. The group of recruits on the far side cheered, patting the recruit on the shoulders exuberantly.

Ramirez climbed down into the pit, helping their injured teammate out. Two recruits at the head of the line helped pull him to ground level.

Carter's face was bloodied, his nose twisted, his lips cut and bleeding. Kaalinda hoped most of the damage was superficial.

Captain Carson bent over the recruit, who was softly moaning as he lay on the ground. She shook her head, then, motioned for the medic who was standing by.

Two of the medics brought a stretcher, gently placing Carter in it, checking for broken bones. One stood, pulling his radio from the loop in his belt, radioing the clinic. The second medic worked to stabilize Carter in the stretcher.

Kaalinda watched them carry Carter to the waiting medical transport. She did not like the worried looks on their faces; those looks made her worry, too.

The next two recruits entered the pit.

Listening, Kaalinda tried to determine which recruit was which, but the shouts and thuds were indistinguishable. She watched the faces of the Major and the Captain instead.

Once again, Major Denison's team won.

The loser didn't have to go to medical, though. He had taken the blows much better and only needed to rest on the sidelines.

The next two recruits entered the pit.

Kaalinda was now at the front of the line and could watch the action firsthand. Looking down, she saw smears of red on the rough surface of the concrete. In a couple of places, the blood pooled in tiny hollows on the floor of the pit.

Each combatant held a four-foot long pugil stick, with hard rubber balls on each end. These were used to hit your opponent and protect yourself from being hit.

A recruit from a different company, farther along in his training, acted as referee. He wore the same uniform as the combatants, but had a red bandana tied around his left bicep. Kaalinda could see gray sleeves extending out from his camouflage jacket.

The refereeing recruit was wearing his suit.

He checked that each recruit was ready to begin, then nodded.

The two opponents circled, staying apart, carefully balancing their weapons in front of them at waist level.

Watching, Kaalinda leaned forward to see more clearly. Ramirez gently pulled her back from the edge. She shrugged his hand away. Ramirez backed up, hands' palms up facing her.

Captain Carson frowned at them once, then looked back to the fighting.

The opposing team's recruit made a move, wildly swinging his weapon. It was easily deflected. The two men sparred, until one landed a hit that knocked the other to the ground.

Smiling, the Captain and Ramirez assisted the victor from the pit. Slapping hands ensued, congratulations meted out. Their side had finally won a battle.

Kaalinda turned to climb down the ladder, carefully placing her foot on the rung.

At the bottom, she turned to pick up her weapon, and came face to face with her opponent—Wilkins.

The hate in his gaze made Kaalinda cringe inside. Looking up at Major Denison, she caught his smile.

Stooping to retrieve her weapon, she kept wary eyes on her opponent. She knew he would be out for blood; after all, he had failed in the artificial jungle. Kaalinda wasn't sure how he had gotten out of going to the brig, but he had rejoined the battalion after only a day out at medical.

Nodding to the referee, she bent her knees, balancing her body weight on the balls of her feet. She faced Wilkins, keeping her head lowered and her body ready to move.

Wilkins circled to his left.

Kaalinda moved to her left, keeping herself a good two feet from the walls. She didn't want to let herself get pushed into the hard concrete.

Glancing down to avoid a puddle of blood that could make her slip, she almost missed Wilkins' first thrust. She caught it out of the corner of her eye, just a blurred movement.

Instinct helped her react.

Nostrils flaring, she brought her own stick up, turning it perpendicular to the floor to parry. She felt the impact surge through her arms, all the way to her shoulders and back. She rallied her own thrust. Wilkins easily knocked her stick out of the way.

They circled once again.

"You're fucked, MacReady. Do you hear me?" Wilkins spoke in a low, guttural whisper. "When I'm through with you, you'll be black and blue. And once you're back in the compartment, no one will be able to help you. You're mine, MacReady, all mine."

Kaalinda tried not to listen. She knew he was trying to rattle her, but she also knew he intended to do exactly what he said he wanted to do.

"C'mon, Cunt! Give it up. You know you want to." Wilkins kept up his constant badgering.

The referee stepped between them, signaling Wilkins that he was out of line. Wilkins nodded and stopped talking, resorting to mere glaring and baring of teeth to intimidate her.

Then, he made another move, lunging forward, one end of his weapon pointed at Kaalinda.

Kaalinda jabbed, swiping the stick away with one end of her own, then driving in and up with the lowered end. Her weapon made contact with his groin.

The screech from Wilkins sent shivers up her spine and made the referee wince. He didn't halt the fight, though. Wilkins waved it off, backing away to regroup.

Kaalinda knew he would be pissed now. It felt good, though. That one hit had sent a thrill of pleasure through her. Now, she wanted more. She was tired of Wilkins, tired of always being on the defensive.

Wilkins stood, his weapon held at a diagonal in front of him, slightly stooped at the waist. He took a few seconds to recover, gasping deep breaths of air.

"You're dead, MacReady. D-E-A-D!" This last was screamed.

Kaalinda had no doubt that he meant it.

The referee signaled for them to resume fighting.

Before Wilkins could mount his own attack, Kaalinda charged forward, her weapon balanced in front of her.

Wilkins tried to retreat, but he had backed himself into a corner and had nowhere to go.

Kaalinda raised her weapon and swung it down, like an axe. It made full contact with is head.

Wilkins crumpled to the floor, blood pouring from the crack in his head.

Kneeling, gasping for breath, Kaalinda didn't see the damage she had done. Her eyes were closed tight. Her hands let loose of her weapon, and it rolled to the side, one end resting in the spreading bank of red liquid.

The referee pulled her back and to her feet. Someone pushed her to the ladder, and someone else pulled her to ground level, where she lay on the ground, breathing heavy.

Around her, Kaalinda felt the rush of movement. A cool hand touched her neck and a low voice counted her pulse.

The squeal of rasping medal sounded next to her. Something heavy was placed on the metal stretcher.

"He's dead."

Kaalinda didn't know who said the words, but it was like a knife slicing into her soul. She had killed—on purpose. She'd gotten a thrill from it, enjoyed it even. Had wanted to do it.

She had come here to learn how, but the reality was devastating in a way she had never imagined.

Moaning, she flailed her head from side to side. "No," she whispered, hoping someone would hear. That someone, please say it was a mistake.

"It's okay, MacReady. It's okay." The voice belonged to Ramirez.

She flinched, rolling away from his comfort. She pulled herself to her hands and knees, trying to stand.

"Whoa, girl." Captain Carson steadied her, wrapping her strong harms around Kaalinda's shoulders. "Take it easy. You need to stay still."

Kaalinda blinked her eyelids, trying to focus on the swarm of moving bodies. Two patrol officers, their badges gleaming in the sun, were taking statements.

"He said he was going to kill her. He'd tried twice before. It was self-defense." Ramirez spoke to the nearest officer, who nodded at his statement.

"Yes, we know about that. Your Captain submitted paperwork on both incidents. We're ruling it accidental, self-defense." The officer closed his electronic pad, looking up at Kaalinda. She recognized him as one of the officers from that long-ago morning in the brig.

Kaalinda swallowed. She knew he recognized her. After all, she was one of the few women currently training.

Ramirez was speaking again. "If you knew he wanted to kill her, how come he came back to the battalion?"

The soldier looked at Ramirez, then at Kaalinda. "In case you didn't realize it, this is the military. You're learning to kill and you're learning how not to be killed. I'd say MacReady here has been studying pretty hard."

The soldier looked back to Ramirez, who remained silent.

"I just don't want to hear of any more incidents involving Recruit MacReady. Is that understood?"

Kaalinda nodded, relief making her knees weak. She sagged against the Captain, her eyes rolling back in her head, and fainted.

23

CHAPTER 23

8 JAN 2115

KAALINDA SAT IN THE hard chair across the desk from Captain Carson, her hands folded in her lap, plucking at the fabric of her baggy shorts.

"I wanted to speak to you before the Major came in." The Captain leaned back in her chair, the joints squeaking as she tipped it back on two legs. "What happened yesterday..." She let the words trail off.

"I understand ma'am. When will I leave to go to the brig?" Kaalinda couldn't look the other woman in the face.

"You're not going to the brig, MacReady. The decision of the patrol officers on site has been upheld."

Kaalinda passed her tongue over her dry lips. "What are they going to do to me?"

Captain Carson popped her chair back to the floor, the legs thumping against the threadbare carpet of the office. "They aren't going to do anything to you, as long as you aren't a rebel.

Kaalinda brought her head up, staring at the deep brown eyes of her senior officer. "Rebel? You mean a spy for the rebels?" Her voice rose, gaining a shrill edge that made her wince.

Captain Carson frowned, her gaze sharpening on Kaalinda.

She couldn't avoid the direct gaze. Swallowing hard, she winced as her faint gulping sound seemed to echo loud in the silent office.

"MacReady?" Captain Carson rose to tower above her, leaning over the desk.

Kaalinda remained silent.

"MacReady, if you know something, tell me. It's not worth it to protect someone whose only reason for being here is to eventually kill you and every other recruit here."

Kaalinda closed her eyes, taking a deep breath, then, whooshing it out through her nose.

"Maybe it was Wilkins. He did try to kill me." Kaalinda opened her eyes, watching the reaction of the Captain.

Captain Carson sat back down in her chair. "Wilkins wasn't the traitor. He was a government spy, looking for a traitor. He went after you because he thought he'd found him, or rather, her." Captain Carson leaned forward on her desk, her arms crossed. "Was he right?"

"No!" Kaalinda yelled her denial, jumping from her chair to pace the office. "No." She spoke more calmly the second time.

"It is odd that you were drafted for training. You're not the usual recruit."

Looking at the Captain, Kaalinda stared her down. "Wouldn't that fact make me the least likely candidate to be a traitor?"

Captain Carson shrugged, leaning back in her chair.

Kaalinda scrubbed her fists into her eyes. She was tired. She hadn't slept much last night, after returning from medical. They had wanted to observe her after her fainting spell.

God! How embarrassing. She'd gone down in front of the entire battalion.

The horror of yesterday flashed before her now, as it did every time she closed her eyes. Tears threatened. She took a deep breath, struggling for control.

Kaalinda turned away from the Captain. She could hear the soft rustle from the chamber just outside the office. Ramirez and the section-leaders were getting up. Soon, the rest of the battalion would be awake.

Whispered voices remarked on the thin strip of light that escaped beneath the door. A tentative knock interrupted Kaalinda's morbid thoughts.

"I'm in here." The Captain didn't yell, but made sure her voice was loud enough to be heard.

"Yes, Ma'am." Ramirez answered and moved away, his feet shuffling in flip-flops across the tile.

Something must have shown in Kaalinda's stance, a faint flicker of wayward emotion as she jerked at this voice.

"My God!" The expletive was whispered. Captain dropped back into her chair, her hands dangling over the sides of the armrest.

Kaalinda stared at the astonished look on the Captain's face. She didn't speak, but sat back down in the hard plastic chair. She crossed her ankles, folded her hands in her lap, and waited.

Captain Carson opened her mouth, then shut it again before speaking. She shook her head, looking at Kaalinda the whole time.

Slowly, Kaalinda nodded.

Revenge.

She had sought revenge for the death of her brother, the destruction of the hope for her family. She had wanted to mete out punishment with her own hands. She had thought it would be later though, during a skirmish between the government and the rebels. She would have been the winning force, killing as many of the rebels as possible.

Instead, it was all much easier. There was no battle, no blood. With a simple nod, she sealed the fate of the man who had admitted to being a rebel, to even being there during the attack.

It didn't make her feel better, though. Why didn't she feel the same rush and thrill that she had experienced when she'd hit Wilkins during combat? Where was the satisfaction?

It's not like she believed his story that it was the Government that had done the damage.

Instead, she felt the same horrible black hole opening before her that had sucked her in after Wilkins' death. He had been trying to kill her and she had mourned him.

Gritting her teeth and gripping her hands tight, Kaalinda betrayed Ramirez, the man who had once been a friend, when no one else was, but who she now knew was an enemy.

"He's a rebel." Kaalinda whispered the words, leaning forward to make sure the Captain could hear. She didn't want anyone else eavesdropping. "He told me. He was at the attack in the Aurora Sector."

Captain Carson narrowed her eyes, leaning back. "How do I know you aren't the rebel who was in the attack."

Meeting her direct distrustful gaze, Kaalinda responded. "I was in the Capital—taking the final standardized curriculum test—when it happened. My parents—my whole family—lived in the Aurora Sector. My brother died in the attack."

Memories of her childhood with Pol rushed at her, and weakened by recent events, Kaalinda let the tears fall.

Captain Carson nodded, picking up her portable comms at the same time. After punching in a few numbers, she placed the device near her ear.

"I know who the mole is. Send up the officers."

Without waiting for a reply, Captain Carson turned off the comms and stood up. "Wait here."

Kaalinda nodded. She pulled her feet up, tucking them beneath her, and wrapped her hands around her knees. She rested her cheek against them, staring blindly at the door that closed with a soft click after the Captain.

All was silent for a minute.

Kaalinda listened hard for the telltale sounds. All she could hear were the recruits walking around, talking low. She heard a comment about the Captain, regarding which side of the bed she'd gotten up on that morning, but nothing else.

The creak of the main compartment door being opened cut through the silence, and Kaalinda heard the voices of the patrol officers. All other voices had stopped.

"Where is Ramirez?" Captain Carson's question bounced off the walls it was so loud.

Kaalinda couldn't hear the reply. A buzzing started in her ears. She felt sick. "What have I done?" She whispered to herself. "Oh, God, what have I done?"

She rocked in the chair, a slight, comforting motion.

The scrape of metal against the floor indicated that Ramirez was not going quietly. Shouts and thuds followed.

"What the hell is going on in here?" Major Denison's voice halted the commotion for a moment.

"Recruit Ramirez is a rebel." Kaalinda didn't recognize the deep voice, so it must have been one of the officers.

"Get him out of here." Captain Carson's voice was cold.

The thumps and bumps started once again, followed by the thud of the door closing. Silence loomed heavy over the compartment. Kaalinda could hear faint scuffles as recruits surely shifted on their feet.

"Get on with your routine. We leave for chow in ten minutes." Major Denison took charge.

Their footfalls grew closer, pausing just outside the door to the office.

"Who's the informant?"

There was a slight pause before Captain Carson quietly answered the Major's question.

"Recruit MacReady."

"And you believed her? She's probably the rebel herself, trying to throw the scent in another direction."

"No," the Captain's voice rose slightly, "her story checks out. Her brother was killed in the attack at Aurora. She wouldn't have had anything to do with that. Her father is a staunch supporter of the government. She's telling the truth."

"Carson..."

Captain Carson cut him off. "Major, I think you should remember that you gave permission to

Wilkins to harass her, even kill her. I think you need to watch your step."

"What do you mean?"

The knob turned. "I submitted a lot of paperwork about MacReady. Including how she saved the life of a fellow recruit. That doesn't sound like the actions of a rebel, does it?"

"No."

"And yet you were willing to let Wilkins kill her anyway."

There was silence on the other side of the door before it swung open.

Kaalinda jumped to attention, heels together, hands at her sides. She stared straight ahead, avoiding the gaze of her battalion commanders.

"You're dismissed, MacReady. Get ready to go."

"Yes, Ma'am." Kaalinda saluted, her hand bumping into her forehead in her haste. Turning, she marched out of the office and found her clothes, still hanging on the post of her rack.

She pulled on the trousers, zipping them before they were all the way up. Thrusting her arms toward the sleeves, she missed the first time, struggling to get the job done as fast as she could.

She didn't want to think.

Carter stood across from her, leaning back against his rack, arms across his chest.

Meeting his gaze, Kaalinda was surprised to see the hatred burning in their gray depths. Kaalinda stopped midway through buttoning her jacket. Realization was swift.

Ramirez and Carter had been fast friends, almost as if they had known each other before coming here.

There might be more than one rebel in her battalion.

Carter straightened, crossing the room slowly. He stopped when he stood directly in front of Kaalinda.

Pointing one finger at her, he whispered. "Watch yourself, MacReady. You don't know what you're getting into."

Kaalinda stared a moment, then spoke. "I think you're the one who doesn't understand, Carter. They already knew. They were looking. None of us would have gotten through until they found him."

Carter sneered. "Ramirez should have let Wilkins finish you off. It would have been so simple. They all thought it was you."

"No, they didn't. Captain Carson knew it wasn't me."

"Wouldn't have mattered once you were dead. Command would have been satisfied." Carter pushed her into her rack.

"Hey!" A nearby recruit intervened. "What's going on?"

"Nothing to be concerned about."

Kaalinda and Carter waited for the recruit to move away.

"Watch yourself, Carter. You don't want to give yourself away. Then, they'd have two rebels in the brig, instead of just one."

Carter pushed her once more, then stalked back to his rack, pulling the bottom edge of his jacket down. He picked up his starched cover from the top of his locker, then smashed it onto his head.

He took his place in line, standing at parade rest.

Kaalinda finished dressing, glancing over at Carter, over at all the recruits standing in line, wondering who else in her battalion was a rebel.

Shrugging her shoulders, Kaalinda placed her own cover on her head, and took her place. She wasn't going to worry about it. At least, not right now.

24

CHAPTER 24

15 JAN 2115

KAALINDA STARED PAST THE gate, through the twined wire that shielded the outside from those within the compound. Her suit felt heavy on her body, like thick wool rather than smooth thin silk.

It was cool, the breeze giving Kaalinda goosebumps, making her shiver. Her suit responded, increasing the temperature of her skin by one degree. The small display appeared before her eyes, indicating the step it had taken.

The heaviness probably had something to do with her mood. Her thoughts had been in turmoil since two days ago, when Ramirez had been arrested and charged with treason.

She had stood by, listening while the military police had escorted him from the barracks compound. She had stared at the ground, listening to the low whispers of her battalion mates.

No one had spoken about it since.

Some small part of Kaalinda wished she had not let her anger get the better of her good sense, wished she had kept her mouth shut.

She should be glad. After all, this way, he was getting punished for the crimes against her family. That was why she had wanted to come here, after all—to learn how to avenge her parents, to learn how to kill those responsible for their deaths.

She just wasn't sure he was the guilty party.

What if he had been telling the truth? That the resistance hadn't attacked the Aurora Sector? That it had been the Government? That the Government was lying to blame the rebels? Did the blame ultimately fall on the military she was now a part of, and the government her father so faithfully supported?

Shaking her head, Kaalinda marched past the closed gate. It wasn't locked; this was the gate used by officials leaving and returning to the compound after sunset.

The breeze swirled along the dusty ground, stirring the fine sand into tiny eddies. Thunder rumbled in the distance, dry lightning responded, lighting the horizon for a split second before fading away.

She listened to the coming storm, hoping her relief would arrive before it did. The faint odor of ozone drifted through the air. The storm was closer than she had first thought.

She glanced down at her watch, the strap tight around her left wrist. It was hard to see in the darkness, the light from the solitary lamp above the gate lost in the dust-filled air before reaching the face of her watch

Leaning into the dim light, Kaalinda squinted down at the timepiece. She thought the numbers read 2340. If that was correct, her relief should be there any minute.

In the distance, Kaalinda heard a faint whine—a siren.

The hair rose on the back of her neck. It was the warning that a prisoner had escaped from the brig.

Ramirez?

Kaalinda glanced at the open gate. It was the obvious choice for an escape route from the compound. The only trees of any substance grew just outside this gate, and it was never locked. Kaalinda wasn't sure it was even capable of being locked.

Did Ramirez know of its existence? Kaalinda tried to remember if Ramirez had still been with the battalion when they had been briefed on guard duty. She couldn't remember.

Executing an about-face movement, Kaalinda retraced her steps, back to the other side of the gate. Turning, she stood once more at attention, her heavy laser propped carefully over her right shoulder.

She tested the weight of the laser with her hand, practicing the swift movement that would bring it to her side, then in front, ready for firing.

A slight sound, whispered from the dark, caught her attention, and she turned. Kaalinda stared into the darkness, peering into the swirling dust in front of her. She couldn't see anything.

Probably just your imagination, she chided herself. The faint blare of the siren continued in the distance. *The noise of the siren is spooking you. Your relief will be here any moment now, and you'll be able to go back to the barracks and sleep.*

Kaalinda crossed the front of the gate once more, glancing in the direction of the noise. She heard it again, louder this time, closer.

"Walken? Is that you?" Kaalinda didn't think Walken, her relief, would play with her like this, but she couldn't be sure. Some members of her battalion had weird senses of humor, and others just plain disliked her, still.

"Walken, if that's you, I'll shoot you when you come out!"

Kaalinda stood silent.

Alert now, she readied her weapon, pulling it from her shoulder and steadying it in her grasp, resting it against her hip. She switched the setting to stun.

From the depths of the shadows, Kaalinda saw a figure move, furtive, crouched low to the ground, hiding. Thunder rolled once more, the lightning pricking the sky before the last rolling rumble had faded.

Kaalinda's stomach tightened, her muscles tensed. It was too tall to be Walken. Adrenaline pulsed through her veins. Her breathing quickened. She bent her knees, moving into a semi-crouch, readying her body for imminent attack.

The suit responded. In front of her eyes, a small display appeared. All her vital statistics flashed momentarily before her eyes—body temperature, pulse, heart rate.

It's Ramirez.

A tiny voice inside her head spoke to her. Kaalinda knew it was her suit. She hadn't needed it to tell her, though. Who else would be skulking around inside the compound this late at night?

"I can see you." She didn't shout, but her voice carried through the still air.

The figure stopped its movement.

Kaalinda shifted, adjusting the weapon in her hands. Sweat made her grip loosen, her palms becoming slick. Sand stuck to her skin, the hard grains biting into her palms.

Balancing the laser in one hand, she swiped her palm along her leg. The suit lapped up the water like a thirsty dog, and the wet was gone. Dry sand grains fell to the ground.

Returning her hand to the weapon, Kaalinda swallowed. "Come out where I can see you."

The figure paused, then moved forward, slowly.

Moonlight fell across his face five feet from Kaalinda.

Ramirez looked haggard. Stubble covered his chin and a dark bruise covered his left cheek, a scabbed-over cut on display on his right. His clothes were wrinkled and dirty, a tear cut through his jacket and shirt over his right shoulder. On his skin, Kaalinda could see the red line that marked the path of whatever object had made the cut.

Resting against his thigh was an unfamiliar weapon.

Kaalinda frowned. "What's that?" She indicated the weapon with a quick jerk of her head.

Ramirez shrugged. "Some experimental weapon I found inside after I knocked out my guard." He looked down at the weapon, turning it over in his hands. "I'm not sure what's so special about it. I guess I'll find out eventually."

Kaalinda watched him.

He stood still, waiting.

After a minute, Ramirez shifted on his feet. He drew his left hand to his waist. "Are you going to shoot?"

Kaalinda stared a moment before answering. "Will I have to?"

"Yes."

"Why?" Kaalinda's voice was a whisper.

Ramirez shrugged, wincing. "Maybe I deserve it. I was in the Aurora Sector when it was attacked. I did nothing to try to help. I just ran away."

Kaalinda snorted. She shifted the laser off STUN, back to KILL. Steadying the weapon, her finger moved to squeeze the trigger. Ramirez did not wear a protective suit; nothing would stop the laser blast.

Ramirez closed his eyes. Sighing out his last breath, his nostrils flared with the force of the air.

Kaalinda hesitated, a faint mewling sound stirring from the bottom of her stomach, escaping through tense lips. Her suit tingled. Miniature shock waves rippled up and down her spine.

He'd been just a kid. Barely a year older than her when it happened. What could he have done to stop it?

She couldn't move her finger. Inside her head, that little voice whispered, *No No No*.

"Run."

Ramirez' eyes popped open. Dark orbs glistened down on her in the dark, the whites reflecting the luster of the moon.

He raised the strange weapon, aiming at Kaalinda's left shoulder. One brown cocked high into his forehead.

Kaalinda nodded, responding to his silent question.

The momentary burst of blue light was finished before it had really started. Only the fire in Kaalinda's shoulder proved it had been real.

"Oh, God! Red, are you okay?"

Eyes closed, Kaalinda crumpled, falling back to the hard ground. Her weapon fell to the ground next to her, just beyond the grasp of her fingers. She felt Ramirez' warm fingers press against her neck. Struggling to remain conscious, she raised her right hand, grasping his at her neck.

"I'll be fine. I'm in my suit. Get out of here or they'll catch you."

Kaalinda heard Ramirez' harsh whoosh of exhaled breath, felt the fleeting brush of his breath against her cheek, his dry lips. Strong fingers crushed hers in silent farewell.

Then, he was gone.

Kaalinda heard the low moan of the gate open, then close.

The fire in her shoulder spread across her body; the suit attempted to absorb the damage. The surge of energy winged through the fabric of the suit to her shoulder. A cold built up, seeping into the fire. But the fire spread more quickly than the cold, and Kaalinda sank into the darkness.

Once there, she saw Pol, smiling at her, pride glowing from his ethereal features. Kaalinda felt the pride reach out to her, permeate her muscles, her bones, penetrating down to her soul.

Peacefully, she sank into the oblivion.

25

CHAPTER 25

17 JAN 2115

THE BLACKNESS LIGHTENED, SETTLING into a swirling gray of semi-consciousness. Kaalinda could feel the coolness of sheets resting lightly on her skin, but could not make her fingers move to touch them. Her limbs were heavy, weighted down into the softness beneath her.

At least she was no longer outside.

That realization brought her mind into sharper focus, heightening her senses. She was under sheets, resting on what felt like a mattress.

Where was she?

Lemon-scented bleach wafted to her nose, probably from the sheets. What was most peculiar to Kaalinda was the lack of other odors. No wax or mildew, no sweat or other body odor that permeated the air of the battalion chambers; no ammonia or medicine that marked the air at medical.

Just where the hell *was* she?

Low voices reached her ears, then the faint whoosh of a door opened.

At first, she could not decode the gibberish into recognizable words. Concentrating, she pushed the gray mist in her brain aside, creating a tunnel of clarity. The voices traveled through the tunnel. Clear now, she listened.

"At least we know the weapon does affect the armor. A direct to the torso should have killed her, though. We'll have to increase the intensity and make some modifications to have a handheld laser that makes the armor virtually useless."

"I still don't understand what made the difference. Lab tests with the suits had them burning to a gray ash when fired on." Another voice joined the first. "She should have been killed."

"We'll have Simons run some tests."

Direct hit?! Kaalinda stopped listening and struggled through the fuzzy memory of what had happened.

Ramirez! The gate! He had shot her in the shoulder.

Awareness of her injury brought pain. Kaalinda moaned, shifting, trying to move away from the fire alight on her shoulder.

"She's awake. Hit the button."

Kaalinda heard the faint squeak of rubber soles and sensed movement beside her. Soon, she heard the door open once more.

She still could not open her eyes. Fear rolled in her stomach, followed by waves of nausea.

A gentle hand returned to her wrist, fingers and thumb seeking a pulse. "Pulse steady."

Kaalinda urged her body to respond to her commands. *Eyes open! Eyes open!* They still did not respond. Lost in a world of black-gray mists, Kaalinda whimpered.

"Shh." A soothing voice crooned into her left ear, a gentle hand stroked her forehead—a soft, female hand. "Everything will be fine. Rest now." The hand was removed. Instinctively, Kaalinda made to move her head, to follow the warm touch of reassurance.

"Check her temperature." The male voice was obviously in control.

"Yes, doctor." The female responded, her voice moving away. The near-silent slide of an opening drawer drew Kaalinda's attention. The sound was followed by the gentle clink of shifting metal.

"Here we are." The voice was close again. Kaalinda felt the cool tip of a thermometer slide into her ear, instantly hearing the soft beep that indicated it had completed its task.

"There, not too bad." Kaalinda felt a gentle caress as fingers drifted down her cheek.

The staccato tap of computer keys alerted Kaalinda to the presence of a computer in the room. The unit was right next to her.

"There, doctor. I've entered the data into her record."

"Let's take a look at her shoulder." The doctor was to her left now, close. Kaalinda felt his cool fingers on her arms, gently positioning it by her side.

She jumped though, when those same fingers touched her shoulder. They now felt like jagged teeth of ice, biting into the seared flesh of her wound.

Crying out, Kaalinda moved on the bed, her pumping legs futile in their instinctive attempt to run from the pain. She tried to turn away, roll to her uninjured side, but the gentle hands turned into iron weights that grasped her legs, keeping them still. A warm weight covered her upper body and right arm, pinning them to the bed.

"No!" Kaalinda screamed as the teeth once again gnawed at her pain, probing the fire.

Ice should melt in fire, right? The errant thought raced through her darkening mind.

Kaalinda reached out, grasping for the hand of sanity, but it loosened its grip, releasing her. She fell back into the black pit of sleep.

***

She awoke again to the faint rumble of voices. This time, the blackness faded quickly, and she opened her eyes.

She was lying on her back, her head on a pillow. Again, the clean scent of lemon filled her nostrils. Above her, a pristine white ceiling smiled down. The brightness, fed by an open window to her right, made her wince.

Slitting her lids, she let her eyes adjust before seeking out the speakers.

Everything in the room was white. The ceiling, the walls, the cabinets, and the sheets. Even the speakers appeared to be covered with white.

There were two figures wearing white lab coats in front of the white door. Their trousers were also white, and white masks and caps obscured their faces and covered their heads.

"So, what do we do now?" The figure speaking was tall. He would have to duck to clear the doorway when he left. The movement of his chin made his white mask shift.

"Move up the development of the weapon, I suppose. Essentially, it's been tested and it can put them out of commission. We can work on getting a new prototype made, one that will do more damage. Something smaller, maybe. Get it into production and to the troops before the rebels can learn to use the technology."

The shorter man had a deeper voice, and his mask didn't move as much when he spoke. A spark of recognition lit deep in Kaalinda's mind, but she couldn't remember where she had heard the voice before.

"So, have they found the fugitive or our prototype yet?" The tall man leaned his thin frame against the door jamb, arm outstretched, the other balanced on his hip.

"No." The shorter man shook his head. Kaalinda thought she saw a trace of dark hair beneath his shifting cap. "I don't expect they will. He'll hold on tight to that laser, do whatever is necessary to get it to his people. He knows what it can do, what we'll be able to do with it."

Both men turned their heads toward the door. A soft click signaled that someone was entering.

They moved away so the door could swing wide.

Kaalinda closed her eyes, feigning sleep.

So, Ramirez had succeeded with his escape? A wash of warm relief filled her entire being. It was good that he was safe.

"Excuse me, sirs." It was the female voice once again.

Kaalinda heard the rattle of a wheeled cart being pushed into the room. It stopped somewhere near the end of the bed. Squeaky footsteps moved to the right. The brightness outside Kaalinda's lids dimmed. A cool hand touched her forehead, then moved to cup her cheek.

Kaalinda decided it was time to wake up.

Groaning, she shifted her head from side to side, slowly. She grimaced for real when the movement pulled at the dressing covering her damaged shoulder.

Opening her eyes, Kaalinda looked into the gaze of the owner of the female voice.

She had blue eyes.

Kaalinda returned her stare for a moment before frowning. "Where am I?" Her voice rasped out the words, her tongue lethargic, slurring the sounds together.

"You're in the research hospital. They brought you here when your relief found you injured."

The woman lifted Kaalinda's head, rearranging and fluffing her pillow. Setting Kaalinda's head back down, she straightened the sheets, smoothing out any wrinkles, adjusting the white knit blanket, folded and draped precariously on the corner at the foot of the bed.

Kaalinda watched the quick, automatic movements. The woman was slim, with long blonde hair pulled back into a neat roll. She too wore a white uniform—a short-sleeve tunic tucked into a slim, a-line skirt that stopped just above her trim knees.

"I'm your nurse. The name is Bromley." The nurse continued around the bed adjusting, tucking, and dodging the two men who stood silent nearby. She pulled a bed table over to Kaalinda.

"If you need me for anything, just press that little button, right there." She stopped to point to a blue button on top of a small white box attached to the side of the bed, near Kaalinda's hand. "There's one on either side."

Kaalinda looked to her left and right, seeing the buttons were within easy reach.

"It will ring me." She patted another small white box attached to her belt. This box had a small display on it.

"The doctor will check you over later this morning, so we'll try walking and the bathroom after that. Right now, it's time to eat." She indicated the cart she had wheeled in earlier.

Kaalinda had forgotten about the cart, and now focused her gaze on its shiny, metal surface. She was surprised to find that she was hungry, her stomach grumbling about its lack of sustenance.

Bromley removed the warming lid, and Kaalinda's stomach ceased its grumbling, and downright screamed to eat. The tempting odor of butter-brushed biscuits and fresh-squeezed orange juice made her nose rejoice. The tray was filled with scrambled eggs, seared ham slices, fresh-cut melon, and strawberries. Creamy milk and amber-colored juice rested in frosty glasses. Fluffy white biscuits steamed on the side. Kaalinda hadn't seen food like this since before her arrival at training. Hand shaking, she tentatively reached out to the tray, attempting to rise onto one elbow to reach the plate.

"Here, here. Don't overdo. Let me raise the bed for you." Bromley moved to a rectangular wall panel covered with small buttons. "Let me know if I move it too fast."

The head of the bed rose slowly, propping Kaalinda closer and closer to the aromatic wonder in front of her. Her whole being concentrated on the food. She forgot all about her shoulder.

Her stomach threatened revolt. Before the bed had stopped moving, Kaalinda had grabbed the fork with her right hand and was tasting the creamy eggs.

They melted in her mouth.

Tears gathered beneath her lids, threatening to spill from her eyes. The exquisite sensation of good food in her mouth was almost more than Kaalinda could bear.

Bromley turned to the two men who watched in silence, waving her hands at them to usher them from the room.

"You can question her later. Right now, she needs to eat. Doctor's orders."

Reluctantly, the men left, glancing back at Kaalinda, who sat in bed, enthralled at the opportunity to eat real food.

26

CHAPTER 26

20 JAN 2115

K AALINDA STARED AT THE pristine gray dress uniform hanging from the hook on the door of her room. Someone had already pinned her nametag over the left breast pocket, the rectangular silver tab perfectly aligned with the edges of the pocket.

A couple of ribbons adorned the top of the left pocket, awards for completing tests during training. The bright-colored ribbons seemed to pop out from the dull gray of the shirt.

Sharp pleats creased each pocket, continuing down the shirt to the bottom. Kaalinda knew there were three equally sharp ones running down the back of the shirt.

Polished black patent shoes were tucked next to the table, a rolled black sock peeking out from each. Her cover, complete with silver trim, sat on the table, stiff from being well-starched.

It waited for her.

Kaalinda sat, propped up in bed, her right hand holding on to the forearm of her left.

She felt nothing.

It no longer hurt. She had medication that took away the pain in her shoulder, but left her with no feeling in her arm at all. No movement, either. She moved to the edge of her bed, her feet slipping to the cool tile floor. She curled her toes, resting briefly before standing.

Weakness rushed through her legs when she put weight on them. She sat back down. Blood rushed through the veins in her legs, sending tingles along the nerves. Once the tingling had stopped, she tried to stand again. This time, her legs stayed strong, and she moved to the uniform. From her standing vantage, she could see the white tee shirt and underclothes neatly folded on the chair by the table.

Breathing deep, Kaalinda released the closures on her bed gown, letting the thin material sink to the floor. Stooping, moving slow so as not to make the blood rush to her head, she picked it up and draped it over the back of the chair.

The underclothes were awkward to put on with on with only one arm and hand. She gave up on wearing the bra and settled on just wearing the tee shirt. She was built small, so it shouldn't be much of a problem.

Sitting on the chair, she pulled on her socks then tugged the stiff-pressed pants on, rolling side to side to work the fabric up and over everything. The fit was loose, skimming what was left of her curves, emphasizing her muscularity.

She stood up when a squeak indicated that the door was opening.

Dr. Simons entered the room. Seeing Kaalinda half-dressed he apologized and made to back up.

"It's okay, Doctor. I'm pretty much used to it now, and you've seen much more of me."

Dr. Simons cleared his throat. "Yes, well, mhmm..."

Kaalinda continued dressing, ignoring the doctor. She placed her damaged arm in the sleeve, then pulled the shirt up and around her shoulders, contorting a little to get her right arm in the other sleeve.

The buttons were a pain in the ass, but she managed.

"Ahmmm...do you need help?" Dr. Simons moved toward her, one hand outstretched.

Kaalinda glared him back. "I don't need any help, thank you. I'm fine."

The doctor nodded, moving away. He paced, taking a few short quick strides before turning around and moving in the opposite direction.

Kaalinda watched, finishing the last button, then slowly tucking her shirt into her pants. The pants zipper wouldn't move; she was just pulling on the fabric with the gray-coated tab. She leaned against the table, using pressure against the edge to hold the fabric taut while she pulled the zipper closed. She had to stand on tiptoe to get positioned properly. She felt relieved when it was done.

She looked around for the belt, but couldn't see one. She moved her cover. There it was, curled up, the shiny buckle in the very center. It was a slightly darker gray than the rest of the uniform, the silver buckle gleaming when struck by light.

Kaalinda looped it through her belt loops; silently counting to make sure it went through each one. The buckle was difficult, so she left it a little loose.

The pants fit well enough not to need the belt, so she wasn't worried.

The shoes were a breeze. They were slip-on loafers, no laces or buckles, the flat tops polished and shining.

Finished dressing and feeling better than she had in a while, Kaalinda turned to the doctor.

"What do you want?"

The doctor stopped his pacing. "We've been running some tests. I thought you might want to learn the results."

"Why the concern now?" Kaalinda stood still, her left arm hanging limply at her side. She placed her right hand on the table, next to her cover.

"I...um...we thought you might have some insight as to why the suit protected you so well. We'd like you to come down to the lab for a few minutes."

Kaalinda watched him fumble for something in the large pockets of his white lab coat.

"Can I see my suit?"

The doctor looked up, stopping his search, one hand still in a pocket. "Why do you want to see it?"

Kaalinda considered her answer, tilting her head to the side. "Curiosity, I guess."

The doctor shrugged. "No harm that I can see. I'll okay it."

Kaalinda indicated that he precede her through the door. She picked up her cover, tucking it under her left arm, up high, the dead weight keeping it wedged in place, and followed.

The halls were empty. No sounds could be heard from anywhere. It was all white walls and white floors, unmarred by scuffs or nicks.

It was very different from the training base.

"Exactly where are we located in regards to the training base?" Kaalinda leaned forward lightly to ensure the doctor heard her questions.

"We're right next to the training base, to the West. I think there is an old bunker, maybe two, between us and it."

Kaalinda was surprised they were so close. She had never guessed anything this modern was nearby. Of course, she had been limited in her movements, and after her experience at medical when she arrived, hadn't imagined the military even had a facility like this.

The double doors to the laboratories swung silent and they passed through. Doors lined both sides of the wide corridor, each with a cipher lock to restrict entrance.

Dr. Simons halted before the third door on the left, blocking Kaalinda's view, and he punched in the code for the lock. After a faint beep, a small green light illuminated above the door.

Dr. Simons pushed the door open, ushering Kaalinda through first.

Kaalinda entered, glancing around the large room until her gaze landed on the raised gurney in the center: her suit.

It was black now, like charcoal; flaky, like singed paper. It had retained the shape of her body, save for a single cut down the middle where they'd lifted her out of it, and lay like a blackened, headless corpse—charred and lifeless.

Dr. Simons stood behind her, silent, waiting.

Kaalinda took a deep breath; the smell hit her: Burnt vegetables or maybe plants.

She shuffled toward it. The left shoulder area was completely gone, crumbled into a black clump of thin, papery material. From there, the damage fanned out, starting darker than black, slowly lightening to dark gray near the feet.

Extending one hand, she paused, glancing at the doctor.

"Go ahead and touch it. We have no more tests to run."

Kaalinda turned back to the suit, her right hand gently touching the right shoulder. It was cold, colder than the air around it. Dead. She trailed her fingers along the chest, watching the furrows left by her fingers in the ash layer. She lifted her fingers, rubbing them together, spreading the flaky residue.

She felt nothing: no spark, no tingle, nothing.

"What did your tests tell you?"

"Not much." Dr. Simons moved to a computer screen, typing in a password before the screen filled with data. "We have no idea why it reacted differently to the weapon than the other suits we tested."

"Had the other suits been in contact with a human? Been worn by someone?" Kaalinda trailed her fingers farther down the suit. At the legs she paused, pressing her fingers tighter against the fabric. Was that a tremor, or was she only imagining?

Kaalinda glanced at the doctor. He was still busily scrolling through the data on the computer. Finding where he wanted to be, he began busily typing on the keyboard.

"I hadn't thought of that." He began scrolling again.

She moved her hand farther down the leg, farther and farther from the wound site. It was definitely a tremor. Near the foot, she felt movement, saw the fabric quiver at her touch and shift beneath her fingers.

Kaalinda bit her tongue to keep from crying out.

The bit of suit curled around one finger, breaking apart from the rest, balling together in her palm. Kaalinda closed her fingers over the small, pulsing bit, squeezing it.

It responded; a small voice in the back of her mind said hello.

Kaalinda placed the small piece of suit in her pocket, careful to appear nonchalant about the movement. She walked away from the suit, moving toward the doctor. "Well?"

"Your test results have been added to the database. Unfortunately, they don't tell us much. You were ideally adapted to use the suit. I wish there were more like you."

"Maybe there are. Maybe you're just looking in the wrong place."

Dr. Simons turned around, eyebrows raised. "What do you mean?"

Kaalinda stared a moment, then that little voice in her mind spoke: Make them hear the message.

"The suit was sent here for a reason, Doctor. Its purpose is not to be a weapon or armor. Something is going to happen. The suits are supposed to protect us from the danger." Kaalinda waited for the tongue-lashing she felt sure she was about to receive.

She didn't get it.

"So, you've heard the message, too?"

Kaalinda frowned. "You know about the message?"

"Yes." Bromley spoke from behind them.

Kaalinda and the doctor whirled around, each letting out a small gasp.

Bromley's approach was slow, her rubber-soled shoes silent on the floor. "We've had other recruits who have heard the message, MacReady. We've tried to get our leaders to listen to them." She shook her head. "It's no use. They don't want to listen."

Kaalinda stared, first at Bromley, then at Dr. Simons, who nodded at her.

"The last one ended up committing suicide. The military psychologist had him believing he was crazy. They took his suit away. We found him dead one morning in his hospital room, dangling from a rope he'd made from his beds sheets."

"And the suit?"

"As it would not accept anyone else, it was used for destructive testing."

Kaalinda looked down. The piece of suit in her pocket shivered, trying to get closer to her. "What are you going to do?"

The doctor shrugged. "Not much we can do. Our hands are tied. The government controls the suits."

Bromley sat on a high stool at one of the lab tables, absently running her fingers over its polished surface. "We're doomed."

Kaalinda looked at her. "Do you wear suits?"

They both looked at her. "No." They answered in unison.

"Start, if you can. The world will need doctors and nurses after the disaster, whatever it is. I think it's close to happening."

Dr. Simon nodded.

Kaalinda turned to leave. "I need to be getting to the inquiry."

"One more thing." Bromley stood up, reaching a hand to delay Kaalinda.

"Yes?" Kaalinda looked down at the hand.

Bromley let go of her. "About your test results..." She stopped, looking at Dr. Simon.

"Your...surgery was reversed. The cauterization of your fallopian tubes." The doctor whispered, watching Kaalinda's face.

Kaalinda's mouth dropped open. "What? How?" She shook her head, confused, looking first at the doctor, then at the nurse.

"We're not sure." Dr. Simons moved forward, grasping her good hand in his in a hearty shake. "I think your suit had something to do with it."

Kaalinda returned the handshake, then reluctantly accepted a hug from Bromley.

"Good luck." Bromley whispered in her ear, giving her an extra hard squeeze. "I'm sorry we brought you into this."

Frowning, Kaalinda leaned back.

Bromley sighed. "You weren't drafted by chance. Dr. Simons is on the panel that reviews the drafting information; he approved you for the draft. Your suit...was one of the originals. We thought," she shrugged, "maybe someone would listen. But no one even realized it was an original. They're too far removed from everything now."

Taking a moment to digest the words, Kaalinda executed a swift pivot and left the room. A guard waited just outside the door. They walked quickly down the corridor.

Kaalinda was ready to meet her fate.

27

CHAPTER 27

20 JAN 2115

KAALINDA SAT IN FRONT of the Board of Inquiry. The board consisted of seven high-ranking officers, three of them women—at least that's what she'd been told. Kaalinda couldn't really tell. They sat behind a semicircular table that curved around the chair she satin, backlit so she couldn't see their faces that well.

Well, except for one...

At the center of the table, General Richards sat staring at her. As Commanding Officer of the base, he was heading up the investigation of Ramirez' escape.

"MacReady, did Ramirez say anything to you before he escaped through the gate you were guarding?" It was the figure at the far right of the table, the voice sounding vaguely feminine.

"Yes, Ma'am." Kaalinda stumbled at the word, unsure. "He apologized for the fact that he was going to shoot me. Spouted something about the right being the way to go. Then he shot me and left."

"Surveillance footage of what happened is dark, but it shows that you raised your weapon, but did not fire." This question came from a deep-voiced

Colonel seated to Kaalinda's left. She turned to face him, keeping her chin up and her neck straight.

"Yes, sir. I was concerned that he might have allies waiting for him outside the gate. I wanted to be certain there was no additional danger. I thought my relief would arrive and we would be able to return him to the brig."

Kaalinda stared at the General. "I assumed that I was safe in my suit. I was under the impression that officials were trying to gain information from the prisoner. I assumed that he should be apprehended alive, not dead."

She was surprised how the lies flew off her tongue.

The officers shuffled papers in front of them. The captain to the left of the General leaned over to whisper into his ear. The General leaned his own head down to catch the words more clearly.

"Our records show that you were on quite friendly terms with the prisoner during training." Once again, the question came directly from the General.

"Yes, sir. I guess we became friends during training. He often helped me with the situation that developed between Recruit Wilkins and myself. I thought he was a good soldier. Once I discovered what he really was, I no longer considered him a friend."

The General and two other figured shifted in their chairs, one clearing their throat.

The throat clearer leaned forward so that Kaalinda could almost make out their features. "Captain Carson stated that you were responsible for him being identified as a rebel."

Kaalinda nodded before vocalizing her agreement. "Yes, sir."

"Why do you suppose he told you about himself? That he was part of the rebel coalition?" The female Major spoke once again.

"Ma'am, though I cannot speak with certainty, I assume it was because he thought we were very close and that I would not turn him in. Because he intervened with Recruit Wilkins on so many occasions, he may have thought I would feel obligated not to tell anyone."

"I see." The female Major sat back in her chair and looked to the General.

The seven were silent a moment, once again reading the papers in front of them, shuffling them a little to straighten them.

"MacReady, you were wounded by an experimental weapon. Do you think Ramirez knew what the weapon was when he took it, or was it just happenstance that he took our newest innovation?" The voice that came from this officer was that of the short, white-shrouded figure that had been in her hospital room.

How was she supposed to answer this question? What did they expect her answer to be?

She watched the figure she knew was a man; he was hunched forward in his chair, leaning over the table, hands folded on his papers.

"In other words," the General interjected, shooting the man an angry glare, "do you feel that gaining the weapon might have been his reason for infiltrating our training operation?"

Kaalinda never took her gaze off the dark-haired man. "No, sir. I didn't ever get the impression that he was here specifically to take something.

He mentioned nothing about a weapon, or even a specific mission, when he admitted to me that he was part of the rebel forces."

"Is that the only reason you believe that?" The dark-haired man continued to ask questions, despite the stares from the other officers at the table.

"No, sir." Kaalinda directed her answer to the General this time, even though he had not asked the question. "He seemed very surprised when he fired the weapon. The look on his face is the last thing I remember before I blacked out."

The General nodded.

Kaalinda thought he seemed satisfied that she was telling the truth.

General Richards leveled a hard stare at her, and Kaalinda's stomach clenched. "Why did you not immediately go to your commanders with the information that Ramirez was a rebel?"

Kaalinda took a deep breath that didn't quite keep the sarcasm from tinging her words. "I was concerned with other things, sir. Recruit Wilkins was attempting to kill me. I was scared about possibly losing the only person willing to stand between me and death."

"MacReady, did you..." It was the man from her hospital room again.

"Thank you, MacReady." The General spoke over the question, tapping his papers on the table to straighten them, and stood. Everyone in the room jumped to their feet at his movement. Leveling a slit-eyed glare at the man who'd harped on the weapon, he addressed everyone in the room. "There will be no more questions about this matter. I'm satisfied with the investigation. Kirkwell," the female Major blinked at the General, "you may submit the final report by 1800 tomorrow."

"Yes, sir."

Kaalinda stood in the center of the room, at attention, in front of the chair she had been sitting in, while everyone else spoke in low tones around her, shuffling papers, stuffing them in briefcases, and leaving the room.

The General was the first to leave.

The dark-haired man watched her, taking his time arranging papers and preparing to leave.

Kaalinda desperately hoped he wasn't going to try to speak to her.

Major Kirkwell nodded once to Kaalinda, then once to the door: the guard stood there, waiting. Kaalinda decided the Major was telling her she could leave.

Kaalinda saluted the Major and turned smartly.

"MacReady..." it was the dark-haired man.

"Colonel Shultz, might I have a quick word with you regarding the report?" Major Kirkwell intercepted the man before he could reach MacReady.

Kaalinda marched to the door, nodding to the guard as she passed.

The guard also turned smartly and followed her.

The hallway was cool. Her stiff dress shoes clicked against the polished wood of the expensive floor. The click of the guard's shoes echoed hers momentarily, and then he was in perfect step with her.

The building that housed the command's headquarters was not like the ramshackle conglomeration that made up the training facility.

Here the walls were marble and real wood; the brass trim gleamed without tarnish.

Kaalinda ran the fingers of her right hand along the gleaming stone, relishing in the smoothness against her fingers. She looked down at her left hand where it hung limp at her side. She couldn't even tell it was there; it had no discernable weight. It was like her arm and a small portion of her shoulder were completely gone.

The guard beside her was silent. She wondered if he was guarding her to keep people away from her, or to keep her away from people. "Are you guarding me?"

"No." The voice was low, almost whispered. "I'm just making sure you don't get lost. This building is tucked away from everything else."

Kaalinda nodded. "Am I heading in the right direction?"

His laughter was as soft as the previous words. "Yes."

Tipping her cover onto her head, Kaalinda awkwardly smoothed the few tendrils of longer hair beneath the brim. She only succeeded in pushing the hat farther back on her head. She pulled it forward again.

The guard stood silent beside her, his own cover already perfectly aligned along his forehead.

Kaalinda pulled her cover forward again, finally satisfied that it was close to where it was supposed to be and pushed herself through the heavy mahogany doors to the outside.

The sun's heat hit her like a wall, searing into her skin, making her blink. The small piece of suit in her pocket reacted to the sudden warmth, stretching and moving. Kaalinda placed her right hand in her pocket, quieting what seemed to be a living piece of fabric.

The brilliant sunlight glared into her eyes. Squinting, she raised her right hand to block it.

"Atten-hutt!" The command startled Kaalinda, and she automatically stiffened into an erect line.

"Pre-sent arms!"

Kaalinda stared.

Standing before her, on the front lawn of the headquarters building, was her battalion, in full dress, saluting her. Dumbfounded, Kaalinda stared into the grinning faces of her friends and fellow recruits.

Captain Carson stood at the one side, also grinning. Subtly, she nodded to the group of soldiers.

Slowly, in perfect unison, the soldiers lowered their inoperative, regimental ceremony rifles, butt down. The new BCO—the irony that it was Carter almost made her laugh!—stood at attention in front of the rest of the battalion and saluted.

Proudly, back straight, Kaalinda raised her good arm, her forearm stiff, and returned the salute.

They dropped their salutes together.

"Well..." Kaalinda didn't know what to say.

The guard behind her laughed. "I guess these fellows will get you out of here and where you need to be. Good luck, soldier." He clasped her on her shoulder briefly—on her left—and Kaalinda wondered that she only felt half of his hand on her.

Kaalinda nodded to him. "Thanks for the escort." She turned back to the battalion. They had broken rank. Some had their guns held in front of them, across their chest; others had them draped carelessly over one shoulder.

"Well," Captain Carson grinned at her, "I see you made it through the board's questions okay."

Kaalinda nodded. "Yes, Ma'am."

"Well." It was funny that Captain Carson seemed stuck on that word, but Kaalinda didn't dare laugh. Though Captain Carson was much friendlier—and fairer—than Major Denison, they were hardly friends. "I guess this is goodbye."

Kaalinda nodded. "I suppose it is." There was no way Kaalinda could continue to serve with only one working arm. "A medical discharge."

"Could have been worse." Tucker had joined them. "For a while there, I thought you might be leaving in a body bag."

Kaalinda nodded. Though she knew he meant it as a joke, she still couldn't laugh about Wilkins—or Hardison. "You, too."

"Couldn't have made it through without you, y'know."

"Yeah, I know." Playfully, Kaalinda punched him in the arm.

"None of us will forget you, Red." Tucker used the name originated by Ramirez, that early day of training so long ago.

It hurt.

Kaalinda swallowed a lump in her throat and licked her lips. "Tucker, please call me Kaalinda. I'm not sure I like 'Red.' Not anymore."

Tucker nodded, lightly punching her on the arm.

"I won't forget you, either—any of you. I'll think of every one of you every time I watch the news and they mention the CFoR." Kaalinda swiped at a tear threatening to fall from her eye. "All of you be careful out there, okay?"

Seventy-odd faces nodded, their expressions solemn.

While everyone had moved closer to her, Carter had remained standing where he had been, but that meant he was now behind them all instead of in front. He nodded slowly to her.

Solemn, Kaalinda nodded back.

Carter understood; she meant him, too. She wished she could have a private moment with him. Ask him if he knew if Ramirez had made it to safety. Wanted to know if they had been sent for the weapon, or if it was just chance. But there was no way that would happen.

There wasn't time. It would be suspicious.

It would put Carter in danger of being discovered.

Shaking herself mentally, Kaalinda spoke to everyone briefly. Soon, it was time to leave; the official transport that would take her to the main transfer point, where she would board another transport for the city and then another back to the Aurora Sector and home.

Kaalinda waved to everyone before boarding the transport, not looking back once aboard. She sat on the far side, looking out the opposite window. The other passengers ignored her; she ignored them in turn.

She was going back. It seemed so long ago that she had left, but it was only shy a couple of months. She would go back to her botany and plants, soil and water and sun. She would concentrate on growing things again, concentrate on living instead of killing.

Honor Pol by rebuilding what he'd wanted to protect, by taking care of their parents as best she could.

She put her good hand in her pocket, feeling that bit of suit wrap itself around her fingers, and smiled.

28

CHAPTER 28

20 JAN 2115

THE EXPLOSION ROCKED THE transport.

Kaalinda fell to the floor, unable to brace herself with only one good arm. Huddled on the floor, she listened for additional explosions.

Others on the transport were also listening.

She could hear their ragged breathing. Raising slightly to look over her seat, she could see them: an older, obviously retired officer crouched on the floor near the back; a young girl who had been visiting her father on base and was returning home to her mother, was sobbing quietly in the aisle; and an active-duty sergeant acting as a courier was guarding the briefcase strapped to his wrist.

Kaalinda looked to the front of the transport; the driver was slumped over the wheel. She could see smoke billowing up from the engine compartment.

How badly was the transport damaged? Should they leave its relative safety?

The smoke increased and Kaalinda could smell burning oil. That was not a good sign.

"We need to get out." Kaalinda stood, still listening for more explosions, wondering what had caused the first one. Had it been something in the engine?

She looked out the side windows, but saw nothing. The base was isolated, a large buffer zone of unpopulated scrub land between it and the nearest city. All that Kaalinda could see was yellow grass and brown-leafed trees. It was nearing autumn, and the leaves had turned brown early, their brief stint of green cut short even further by an exceptionally hot summer.

"Come on." Kaalinda waved for the others to follow her.

"Are you crazy?" The courier stared at her. "We can't leave the transport. How will they find us? We were told not to leave if something happened to the transport."

"I'm sure they meant if it broke down. With the smoke coming out of that engine compartment, I think the engine is on fire."

The sergeant shook his head, pulling the case closer to his chest. "I have my orders."

Kaalinda looked at the retiree. He, too, stayed unmoving at the back of the transport. Kaalinda didn't even bother trying to talk to him; he reminded her of an older Major Denison.

The girl was looking at her, then glancing at the sergeant, then at the smoke that was growing ever thicker. "I'm coming with you." She stood and walked, a tad unsteadily, toward Kaalinda.

"Are you hurt?" Kaalinda reached out her good hand to her, and it was taken quickly, the girl squeezing her hand tightly.

The girl shook her head. "No."

The man at the back stood up. "I'm ordering you to stay put."

Kaalinda looked back at the man. He had his chest puffed out and his chin angled up, looking at her down his bulbous red nose.

"I'm not in the CFoR anymore. And she," Kaalinda pointed to the girl, "never was. Order all you want; we don't have to listen."

At the front of the transport, Kaalinda checked on the driver. She couldn't find a pulse, and blood trickled in a thick red line down his temple. She left him in his seat, taking the first aid kit and a large canteen heavy with what she hoped was water. "Let's go. He's already gone."

The girl swallowed, looking back at the sergeant and the old man. She nodded, taking the first aid kit from Kaalinda and placing the strap over her shoulder.

Once outside, Kaalinda wasn't sure which direction to walk in. "Do you know if we're closer to the base or to the city?"

The girl shook her head. "Sorry, no. This is the first time I've ridden the transport during the day."

"Okay. Which way do you want to go?" Kaalinda didn't really care. Standing where they were wouldn't do any good.

The girl glanced to the right and left and shrugged.

"Let's go left, then. Back toward base. At least we have a better idea of how far it is. We know someone is at the end." Kaalinda took charge, once again taking the girl's hand. They began to walk.

They hadn't gotten far when the transport blew up. Flying debris and pulsating air ripped at them, knocking them to the ground. Instinctively, Kaalinda threw herself over the girl, protecting her as best she could.

The girl was crying now, tears streaming down her face.

Kaalinda wiped her tears, checking over the girl for injuries. She had a cut on her cheek and one on her arm, both caused by her abrupt contact with the road. Kaalinda had been hit on the back with a piece of metal, but couldn't see the damage. Her back hurt, and from the wetness she felt, she imagined that she was bleeding.

"Oh, God, oh God." The girl trembled.

"Shh. Someone will come." Kaalinda wasn't sure if that was true, but she didn't want the girl to give up yet. "Can you tell how bad my back is?"

"Oh, God!" The girl's sobbing became louder and Kaalinda regretted asking her to look.

"It's okay. We need to start moving again." Kaalinda had to lean on the girl a bit; her back throbbed, the pain gaining intensity.

They shuffled down the road, ignoring the blaze behind them. There was nothing they could do for those in the transport now.

"What's your name?" Kaalinda needed something to keep her conscious. She concentrated on talking to the girl, keeping her voice low and calm.

"Tika."

"Tika. That's a pretty name."

"Thanks. What's yours?"

"Kaalinda."

"I like that." The girl looked at her. She only came up to Kaalinda's shoulder, and since Kaalinda was short, that meant the girl was tiny.

"How old are you, Tika?"

"Twelve."

She really was just a kid.

Kaalinda swallowed hard. How was she going to get the girl to safety? She couldn't leave her out here alone, with just a first-aid kit and a water jug.

Rounding a bend in the road, the transport disappeared out of sight. They could still hear the minor explosions as different parts of the engine and body were engulfed in flame, but they couldn't see it anymore.

"Let's stop and open up the first aid pack." Kaalinda was ready to collapse. "We need to check our wounds and clean them up."

"I'm not sure the first-aid kit will have anything for your back." The girl's voice was soft.

"That's okay. I'm more worried about your cheek and arm." Kaalinda nodded to the side of the road. "Let's see if we can find a place in the shade."

Leaning heavily on the girl's shoulder, Kaalinda focused on a spot under the trees. It offered a bit of shade from the sun and a place to sit down.

"Open up the pack; let's see what we've got."

The girl obeyed, opening the pack and setting it on the ground in front of Kaalinda.

Kaalinda couldn't see anything; her vision was getting blurry. This was not good.

She sank to her knees on the ground; her knees hurt at the soft impact. *Damn*. That probably meant that she'd cut her knees up, too.

The girl was going through the pack, reading labels and opening bags. "It's half empty. Half the stuff that should have been in here is missing or already used."

"Is there any antiseptic? You really need to put some on your cuts. I don't want them to get infected."

"What about your back?" Tika looked at Kaalinda, the silver shock blanket in her hands.

"Don't worry about my back. Let's deal with what we can work on. Is there any antiseptic?"

Tika rooted through the pack some more. "Yup."

"Put some on your cuts. Clean them with gauze if there is any and put a bandage on them. There should be instructions for bandaging in there."

The girl did as she was told.

Kaalinda watched the girl's blurry figure beside her.

"All done."

"Good." Kaalinda's voice was weak.

"Are you going to be okay?" Tika's voice sounded far away.

Kaalinda tried to nod, but passed out instead.

29

CHAPTER 29

22 JAN 2115

"WHAT THE HELL IS going on here?"

Kaalinda winced at the loud voice. The pain in her back was dulled and it no longer felt sticky with blood.

"Lower your voice, Ian. I don't want my patient disturbed."

"Patient? That's not a patient, Moira. That's a CFoR soldier. A prisoner!"

"It's an injured person, Ian. I am a doctor. I don't care what side they are on. I don't like people dying when I can stop it."

Dying? Had she been dying?

Kaalinda licked dry lips with an even drier tongue. "Tika?"

A cool hand was placed on her forehead. It reminded her of Bromley. Had they made it back to base? Back to the research hospital?

"She's fine, my dear. Right as rain and sleeping like a baby." The hand moved to her wrist, fingers pressing lightly against the pulse there. "Your pulse is still a bit erratic, but strong. That's a good sign."

The hand patted her on her right arm.

The male voice started speaking again. "Moira, this is ridiculous. She should be in a cell."

"Why should she be in a cell? I assure you, she's not going anywhere anytime soon. She can barely walk with the damage to her back." Kaalinda could tell that the woman was moving around the room; her voice grew faint and then strong.

"Moira..." the man's voice was interrupted by someone else coming into the room.

"Why was the transport blown up? I said we needed to wait for confirmation that the leaked information was correct."

Kaalinda knew that voice. Butterflies whirled in her stomach.

Ramirez was okay.

"And I said we would go ahead. I am in charge here, not you." The man's voice was cold now.

"We're making mistakes. We're being fed the wrong information."

"You don't know that."

"Yes, I do."

"Ian. Leave him be."

"Moira, you can't keep coddling him. He's a grown man now."

"Then treat him like one, Ian. Listen to him. He's making sense."

Kaalinda swallowed and took a deep breath. "Ramirez?" Her voice was so weak, she wasn't sure she had actually spoken.

"What the fuck?" Ramirez' words were hoarse.

A warm, strong hand fell on Kaalinda's arm—her left arm. Her mind was trying to tell her something, but she didn't want to listen. Ramirez was here.

"Red?"

Her arm burned where he touched it.

"Mhmm." Kaalinda tried to nod, tried to open her eyes.

"What the hell is wrong with her?"

"Don't speak to your mother like that!"

"Ian..." The woman's voice went from warning to soothing. "Liam, she was on the transport. She was outside when it exploded—thank God—but something struck her in the back. Marcus and Warren found her and a girl about half a mile from the wreckage."

"Fuck."

"Watch your mouth!"

"Ian..."

Kaalinda snickered. "Is that your dad?" She thought her voice was a little stronger, but wasn't sure.

A short bark of laughter. "Yeah."

Kaalinda giggled. She hoped it was whatever medication she'd been given for her back, but she felt lightheaded. The idea of Ramirez having a dad, and also of having what was evidently a mother, was amusing to her. She just couldn't wrap her mind around the notion.

A deep sigh. "It's not funny."

She could feel his warm breath against her cheek and smiled. It was nice having him close. She didn't want to think about why it was nice, so she didn't. Her brain didn't seem to be functioning as well as it normally did, so it was pretty easy.

She tried to open her eyes. She wanted to see him. To see his dark eyes beneath the dark brows; see him frowning at her. But her eyes wouldn't open.

"Tired."

"Then sleep." A hand—not a woman's hand—brushed her cheek.

"Okay." Kaalinda let out a long breath. "Stay?"

"I'll be right here."

Kaalinda fell asleep to the sounds of another argument. 'Ian' was blasting Ramirez again, talking about something he was supposed to be doing, that he couldn't be shirking it and staying here. And 'Moira', gently patting over her, trying to shush Ian and reassuring Ramirez that Kaalinda was fine and just needed rest.

30

CHAPTER 30

24 JAN 2115

THE NEXT TIME KAALINDA awoke, she was able to open her eyes and keep them open. Her lids still felt heavy, but they didn't keep trying to close on her.

This room was not white. It was a drab green; the walls, the ceiling, and Kaalinda imagined though she could not see it, the floor—though perhaps it was another color. There were no windows. The walls were bare except for an eye chart, its ends curling up a little at the corners.

The single door was closed. It was a slightly darker green than the walls. It had what might be a narrow window in the center of the top half, but it was covered by a brown shade secured by a loop fitted over a small hook.

The bed sheets were white, but not the bright white of the ones at the research hospital, and they were soft, rather than starched, and a bit worn in places. Kaalinda's right hand smoothed over them where they lay on the bed near her hip.

Taking a deep breath, Kaalinda didn't smell bleach, lemon-scented or not. The room didn't smell musty, but the air did smell a little stale—like it had been run through a purifier several times.

The door opened a crack and Kaalinda could hear voices outside. They were arguing; Ramirez and the just-a-bit deeper toned voice of his father. Kaalinda thought they sounded alike. She wasn't sure she should tell Ramirez that. They were disagreeing about a prisoner.

"She should be in a cell!" The voice that Kaalinda thought belonged to 'Ian' shouted.

"She's not a prisoner!" Ramirez shouted back.

"Yes, she is. She's a soldier in the CFoR. That makes her a prisoner. She works for the enemy." The voice had lowered, but was still vehement.

"She's not the enemy. Trust me on this." Ramirez had lowered his voice, too.

"Trust you?" Ian's voice rose once more. "Liam, I trust you. I just think you're too involved here."

"She let me leave, you know. She could have fired and shot me and I would have been recaptured."

"She's the reason you were in there in the first place."

"No." Kaalinda could imagine Ramirez—Liam?—it was hard to grasp that was his first name—facing off with an older version of himself. "I was in there because I was a spy."

"She told them you were."

"I told her I was. When they guessed, she only agreed with them."

"Liam..."

"What if it had been Carter that they asked? Protocol was that if it came down to it, if they suspected, we could turn the other in."

"She's not Carter!"

"She knew about Carter. She didn't turn him in."

"She knew about Carter?" The voice dropped again.

Kaalinda watched the door; it moved in and out with the conversation. She thought that maybe Ramirez was holding the handle while he spoke, swaying it in and out with his words.

"Yes." The door swung all the way open and Ramirez entered. He grinned when he saw Kaalinda. "You're awake."

Kaalinda nodded, not trusting her voice. Her throat and mouth were dry. She tried to lick her lips, and Ramirez frowned.

"Here." He grabbed a water canteen that was strapped to his utility belt, removing the cap before handing it to her.

He was standing on her left. Slowly, she reached across her with her right hand, weakly grasping the canteen. It almost slipped through her fingers.

"Hold up." Ramirez set the canteen on the table next to the bed, then slid one arm under her shoulders, pulling her up into a sitting position. Cranking something on the bed, he then set her back against her pillows. He had propped the head of the bed up for her.

He offered her the canteen of water again, this time holding it to her lips. She sipped awkwardly. Ramirez was tipping it, but not enough for the liquid to easily run out.

"Sorry. I don't want to spill it all over on you. Mum would be pissed."

Kaalinda snorted water.

"Ouch. I bet that was uncomfortable." Ramirez replaced the cap on the canteen and pressed a button on the wall. "Mum will be here in a minute to check on you. Now that you're awake, you'll get to eat."

Kaalinda smiled; her stomach rumbled. "How long?" She couldn't speak the whole sentence.

Ramirez knew what she was asking. "You've been in here for three days. And from what we could get from the girl, it took a day for our guys to find you after the explosion."

"Tika?"

"The girl?"

Kaalinda nodded.

"She's fine. Mum had her patched up quick." Ramirez gave a soft laugh. "She's been shadowing Mum since she got here." He adjusted the pillow behind her head and fussed with her blanket and sheet, making sure they were tucked snugly around her.

A sigh gained both their attentions.

The other man in the room was indeed older, and indeed looked very much like Ramirez. His hair was dark, though touched by gray at the temples, and it was thinning a bit on top. He was tall—though Ramirez might have been a bit taller—and just a bit softer, though still muscular and trim.

"Stop fussing, Liam. You're acting like your mother." The man crossed his arms over his chest and looked sternly at Ramirez.

Ramirez took one step back from the bed, and Kaalinda, but went no farther.

The other man stepped forward, his arms still across his chest. He stood on Kaalinda's right, legs apart, looking down at her. He opened his mouth to speak, but was interrupted by the door opening.

A woman entered, her medium-brown hair bobbed to her chin. She wore glasses and a white lab coat over drab green camouflage. "Ah, the patient is awake."

Kaalinda recognized the voice as 'Moira,' the doctor—and Ramirez's mother.

"You're awake!" Tika skipped into the room.

Kaalinda smiled at her, nodding in agreement.

"I was starting to think you weren't ever going to wake up. I was getting worried." Tika approached the bed, switching from the right to the left when she noticed who was standing where. She stopped next to Ramirez and smiled, reaching out one tentative hand to touch her bare arm.

Kaalinda felt nothing; Tika was touching her left arm. Kaalinda smiled anyway.

"How are you feeling?" Moira had no trouble moving to Kaalinda's right side and pushing Ian out of the way. He grunted, but moved, sighing deeply once more.

"'kay." Kaalinda's voice was still hoarse; she was still thirsty.

"Are you hungry?"

Kaalinda nodded. She was thirsty and hungry.

Moira turned to Ian. "Have someone bring her a tray. Make sure they bring soft, bland foods. She hasn't eaten in three days."

"Moira..."

"Ian," Moira's voice was sharp, "she is my patient. I will say when you can question her."

Ian stalked from the room, slamming the door shut behind him.

Tika glanced to the closed door. "He's mad."

"Yes," Moira agreed. "He's angry, too."

Ramirez's lips jerked up a bit at the corners.

Tika didn't understand.

Ramirez explained. "Mad can also mean insane."

"Oh." Tika glanced to the door again and shifted closer to Ramirez.

Kaalinda tried to shift in the bed, using her good arm to push herself up. Her left arm fell to the side and Kaalinda stared at it.

Ramirez stared at it, too, before gently lifting it back to her side.

Kaalinda winced.

"Does it hurt?" Moira was checking her over, running her hands lightly along her side and neck, but stilled to ask the question. Her fingers pressed hard into Kaalinda's skin and her eyes searched her face.

Kaalinda shook her head. She had felt Ramirez's hand on her arm. It had surprised her, feeling hot and causing pinpricks of sensation along her skin where his fingers had grasped. "I just..." She couldn't explain.

The door opened again. Ian entered, holding the door open while someone else entered behind. That person was also wearing drab green camouflage and a white coat. He was young, though Kaalinda thought he was older than Ramirez.

"I have food—mashed potatoes, scrambled eggs, and banana. Also, some apple juice." The young man was carrying a tray and set it gently on the side of the bed, next to Kaalinda's legs.

Moira moved out of the way and the man pulled the tray's legs down and placed it over her lap. "There you go. Eat slowly. Give your stomach a chance to catch up."

The man left, slipping out the door without saying anything else.

Everyone left in the room stared at Kaalinda.

Kaalinda stared at the food.

Ramirez smirked. "Do you need help?"

Kaalinda scowled. "I don't need your help." She picked up the fork and used it to place a bit of egg in her mouth. Her mouth watered and she swallowed. Her stomach growled in anticipation. She ate some potatoes and a piece of the banana; it had been cut into chucks and placed in a bowl.

It felt like she was eating baby food.

She remembered the last time she had eaten—at the research hospital. The food had tasted wonderful; better than anything she had eaten in the mess hall.

Though simpler fare, this food tasted even better.

Kaalinda groaned half-way through the meal. She didn't think her stomach could take anything more.

Moira smiled. "Easy does it. It will still be there in half an hour. Your stomach might be able to handle a bit more then."

Nodding, Kaalinda put the fork down. Ramirez and Tika had been watching her eat, and now she blushed. But then, she was used to blushing around Ramirez. "How's my back?"

"Healing nicely. That was quite a big gash. Tika said it was from the explosion?"

Kaalinda nodded. "Something hit me from behind when the transport..." She coughed and took a sip of juice, "transport exploded."

"You were lucky to get off in time." Ramirez's voice was gruff.

Kaalinda looked at him. "I couldn't get the others to leave."

"Who else was on the transport?"

"An old man, I think he was retired, and a courier. A sergeant, I think."

"What about the driver?"

"He was already dead." Kaalinda took a breath. "I grabbed the first aid kit and a canteen, leaving one for those staying. The way the smoke was coming out of the engine, I figured it was bad."

Ramirez nodded. "Dad will be interested in the courier. Any idea what he had with him?"

Kaalinda shook her head. "It was a hard-sided briefcase, chained to his wrist. He was holding it to his chest like he expected me to take off with it."

"How big was it?"

Kaalinda shrugged. "It was thicker than a regular briefcase."

Ramirez nodded. His fingers were playing with a wrinkle in her blanket.

Closing her eyes, Kaalinda relaxed back against her pillow.

"Kaalinda?" It was Tika.

"Yes?"

"Thank you for taking me out of the transport."

Kaalinda smiled, her eyes still closed. "You're welcome."

There was movement around her. Moira was still checking her over on her right. Tika was scuffling her feet on her left.

"Why didn't you flinch that time?" Ramirez voice sounded a bit choked.

All movement stopped.

Kaalinda opened her eyes. "What?"

Ramirez nodded to her left hand. Kaalinda looked down. Tika's hand was laid on top of it.

"I didn't know she was touching me."

Ramirez took a deep breath, his nostrils flaring out with the drag of air.

"You can't feel anything in your left arm?" Moira asked the question, frowning while moving around the end of the bed. Gently, she moved Tika back and away, taking her place next to the bed and carefully lifting Kaalinda's hand. She stretched her arm out, manipulating the joints at her elbow and wrist.

Kaalinda shook her head. "It's like it isn't even there. I can't even feel any weight in it at my shoulder."

Moira continued examining her arm.

Ramirez' face was ashen and his throat moved like he was swallowing. He was breathing deeply, his chest moving in and out quickly. He glanced at Kaalinda's face once, then turned and left, swinging himself out the door without saying a word.

"He's upset." Moira spoke with her head down, she was running her fingers over Kaalinda's bicep, pressing in and watching the skin. "He's going to blame himself."

Kaalinda sighed. "I told him to do it."

"Won't make a difference. He fired the weapon."

Tika gasped.

Kaalinda looked at the girl. Her eyes were wide, her mouth open. "He didn't mean to do this damage. We thought my suit would do its job and absorb the hit. It was an experimental weapon."

The girl looked at Kaalinda's arm, biting her lip. "My dad works at the base, doing weapons research. It could be one of his weapons that did that."

Kaalinda looked at Tika. "That doesn't make it his fault, any more than I consider it Ramirez's fault. It was an accident, of sorts."

"I still feel bad."

Moira placed Kaalinda's arm back on the bed. "I think it's a good thing that you feel bad. It means you realize that there are consequences to actions—good and bad."

Kaalinda thought about that night. She really had thought the suit would protect her.

The suit.

The piece in her pocket.

"Where are my clothes?"

Moira looked up from making notes on a paper chart. "They sent it to laundry. The shirt was thrown away—it was pretty much shredded."

Kaalinda bit her lip, trying not to look too anxious. "Was anything taken from the pockets?"

"I don't know, though I'm sure they were searched. I can ask Ian." Moira went back to her chart.

Tika was stroking Kaalinda's arm. Kaalinda watched her. She felt nothing. The only way she knew Tika was touching it was that she could see it.

But she had felt Ramirez's touch. It had caused pinpricks over her skin.

Had he been wearing a suit? Did the rebels have them? Or only the government?

"Moira?"

"Hmmm?" The woman didn't raise her head from the chart.

"Do you have suits? Like the government has?" Kaalinda watched Moira's head come up.

The woman watched her closely, a frown marring her brow. "Why do you ask?"

Kaalinda shrugged. She wasn't sure how much she should tell the woman. "When Ramirez touched my hand..."

Moira cut in before she could finish. "You can call him Liam. I'm not always sure whom you're talking about when you say 'Ramirez.' Ian is called that, too."

"Oh, sorry." Kaalinda sighed. "When ...Liam..." it sounded funny and felt awkward to all him by his first name, "touched my arm earlier, I felt it. It made pinpricks in my skin."

Moira turned from the chart, pencil in hand.

"I was just wondering if the difference was that he was wearing a suit."

The doctor stared at her, then went to the door and hollered out to someone. "Get my son back in here!"

31

Chapter 31

24 Jan 2115

RAMIREZ WAS NOT HAPPY to be back—Ian had come with him. Moira had sent Tika off somewhere.

"What?" Ian asked the question.

"Liam," Moira ignored her husband, "are you wearing a suit?"

"Yes. I am. That's the rule for soldiers around here." His glance at his father was sharp. Kaalinda thought that maybe Ramirez—whoops, Liam—didn't agree with that edict.

"Touch Kaalinda's arm."

Ramirez balked. He stood very still and glared at his mother.

"Go ahead, touch her arm." Moira pointed at the bed and Kaalinda.

He strode to the bed and, taking a deep breath, placed one hand on Kaalinda's arm.

Kaalinda sucked in breath and flinched, trying to jerk her arm away.

Ramirez reeled back, pulling his arm away quickly. "What's wrong?"

"Kaalinda?" Moira came to her other side, placing one hand on her shoulder. "What happened?"

Kaalinda swallowed. "I could feel it."

Moira reached across and placed her own hand on Kaalinda's useless limb. "What about now?"

Kaalinda shook her head. "No. Nothing. It's like always—I can't even tell there's anything there."

"What did you feel when Ramirez touched you. Was it a faint touch?"

"No, like I told you before. There were pinpricks and it felt hot. Like I was cold and he had a fever. Like it could almost burn my skin if he touched me too long."

"Ian, are you wearing a suit?" Moira didn't look at her husband, but continued to watch Kaalinda's arm.

Ian snorted. "Liam said it was regulation for soldiers. Of course, I'm wearing a suit." Ian moved to Kaalinda's left. He seemed to know what Moira wanted him to do without being told. He reached out and placed a hand on her arm.

Tears leaked from the corners of Kaalinda's eyes and she shook her head. "Nothing." Kaalinda took a deep breath and looked away, toward the bare wall. "I just thought...maybe..."

Moira patted her good arm. "I thought maybe it would work, too. Our suits are different from the government suits. And while Liam is wearing one of our suits now, he was exposed to a government suit. That might make a difference."

"How?" Ramirez asked the question, still keeping back from Kaalinda.

"I don't know." Moira sighed. She was making notes on the chart again.

Kaalinda let the tears fall. She didn't even bother trying to wipe them away.

Ian sighed. "I'm going to go see what they've managed to bring in from the transport. There isn't much left of it. Can't imagine our little bomb did that much damage. It wasn't designed to blow it up like that."

Ramirez looked at his father. "I told you. They're playing with us."

Ian looked at his son. "And I'm beginning to believe you. From the remaining debris, you can't tell if there were two or twenty people left onboard when it exploded. Whatever was on it, they made sure it would be destroyed if anything happened."

"Maybe that was why the courier was told not to leave the transport if anything happened." Kaalinda's voice was thick. "That briefcase was chained to him and he was guarding it pretty hard, even from those of us that were supposed to be on the same side."

Ian nodded, looking at her. He addressed her directly. "Are you still on that side?"

Kaalinda didn't know how to answer the question. Was she? She didn't know what side she was on anymore.

When she didn't answer, Ian left, nodding once at Liam and shaking his head at Moira. She was staring at the chart and scribbling furiously on it, completely oblivious to anyone else in the room.

"It hurts? When I touch your arm?" Ramirez moved closer but made sure he wasn't close enough to touch her by accident.

Kaalinda nodded. "It burns."

"I'm sorry." Ramirez whispered.

"Don't be. It means I can feel something. It means that, maybe, my arm isn't completely useless." Kaalinda smiled at him. She didn't want him to feel guilty about her arm. "Look, you could have just shot me straight in the chest. We both though I'd be fine in my suit. You chose to shoot me in my shoulder instead. If I had taken a hit to my chest, I would have died."

Ramirez looked away, Adam's apple bobbing on a hard swallow. "I should have thought it out better. I knew the laser in my hand was different."

"You didn't know how different." Kaalinda shifted up in the bed again. It was awkward using only the one arm, but she glared at Ramirez when he tried to help her.

"Why won't you let me help you?"

"I need to prove that I can do it myself."

"You let my mother help you."

"That's different."

"Why?"

Kaalinda shrugged with one shoulder. She couldn't explain why it was different. Oh, she knew that she didn't want Ramirez to consider her weak or think that she was incapable because of her arm—but she wasn't going to say that to him.

Ramirez sighed. "Why won't you call me 'Liam'?"

Kaalinda stared at him. "You haven't given me permission."

Ramirez glared at her. "You have my permission to call me by my given name."

She grinned at him. "Thanks, Ramirez. I'll remember that and put it under consideration."

Ramirez punched her shoulder. It tingled but didn't burn.

"Can I call you 'Red'?"

"No, you may not call me 'Red'."

"Thanks, I'll take that into consideration."

Kaalinda stuck her tongue out at him.

Ramirez laughed.

"What's this?" Ramirez pulled a small black ball out of his pocket, setting it on her lap. It rolled a bit in a crease in the blanket. "I got it out of your pocket before your stuff went to laundry."

Kaalinda looked down at the hard ball—the bit of her suit that she had salvaged at the research hospital. It wasn't soft and pliant like she remembered. She reached out her right hand to touch it, and it moved. It stretched out toward her hand, elongating and circling her finger.

"What the hell?" Ramirez made to grab for it, and it hardened once more into a ball.

"Don't touch it. You're scaring it when you grab it like that."

"I'm scaring it?" Ramirez glared down at the ball. "What the hell it is?"

"Watch your language or I'll tell your dad."

"Red..." Ramirez growled.

"It's a bit of my suit that survived. I nicked it at the research hospital." Kaalinda touched it again and it softened, once more curling around her finger. Picking it up, Kaalinda watched it flatten and conform to her hand, finally circling it completely.

"A bit that survived?"

"Yeah." Kaalinda looked up at him, smiling. "Isn't it great?"

"What did the rest look like?"

"Like charcoal. And it smelled like burnt cabbage."

Ramirez looked at the blob that pulsed around her hand. "Where did it come from? What part of the suit?"

"The toe. The part farthest away from my shoulder. It was worst at the shoulder, papery and crumbling when I touched it. The closer I got to the toes, the more solid it was until I found where it pulsed, and then this part just broke off and balled itself up in my palm."

"Did your whole suit look like that? Was it that dark?"

"Yeah."

"You must have had one of the older models. The newer models were lighter."

"You didn't notice when we put them on?" Kaalinda kept playing with the piece.

Ramirez flushed. "I had a bit of reaction to seeing you in that white thing we had to wear under them. I didn't dare look at you again."

Kaalinda flushed, the heat spreading across her face and down her neck. She remembered seeing Carter standing across from her with an erection. "I don't think you were the only one."

"I noticed that, too. I didn't like it."

She looked up at him. He was watching the stuff on her hand.

"Wilkins' reaction was the worst. I wanted to punch him 'til he bled out." Ramirez looked up at Kaalinda. "I don't think he liked that he reacted like that. Denison got a kick out of it."

Kaalinda snorted.

The fabric was inching up her arm, winding its way up to her shoulder.

"I don't think my suit will do that. The ones we have here are even lighter than the ones at the base." Ramirez frowned at the fabric just visible beneath the cuffs of his shirt. "I think they changed the formula a lot from the one we acquired."

"How are they made?"

"They're grown. Or rather, the fabric is grown and the suits made out of the fabric."

"Can I see?"

Ramirez raised a brow.

"I was going to be a botanist, remember? This is the kind of stuff I love."

Ramirez stared at her. "I'll see if I can get permission to show you the growing ponds."

He left her alone in the room. The piece of fabric had made its way to her right shoulder and was moving across her chest. Kaalinda left it alone. It wasn't like wearing the whole suit, but she was beginning to understand what Captain Carson had meant by not knowing how you got along without it.

Everywhere that the little bit of fabric touched was warmed. It felt refreshed, like it had been renewed. Kaalinda sighed and rested her head back against her pillows.

Her back was healing well, the wound closed with medical glue that still let infection out. She was still taking a medication for pain, but there was almost no pain between doses now. She was tired of being in bed, wanted to get up and walk around. Even just getting up to go to the bathroom would be good. She was tired of the bed pan, but thought it was better than the catheter at the research hospital.

The door opened, and Moira walked in, followed quickly by Tika.

"How are you feeling?"

"Good."

"They're going to let us go home." Tika was excited, bouncing on her heels. "They're going to get us close to the base and let us walk the rest of the way. We'll have to tell them that we've been walking around in the woods since we left the transport, but I can do that. I told them I wouldn't tell anyone anything."

Moira smiled at the girl. She gave her a one-armed hug and moved to examine Kaalinda.

Kaalinda smiled at Tika. She should be happy to go back. She wanted to go home—didn't she?

"What's that?" Moira was pointing to the blob moving across her chest. It had almost reached her left shoulder.

"It's a piece of my suit. It was the only bit that wasn't ruined."

"What is it doing?" Moira seemed fascinated by the small moving piece of fabric. "I have never seen suit fabric react like that."

"I think it's checking me over. It did that all the time when it was whole."

Moira studied it more. "It isn't hurting you?"

"No. In fact, once it has moved past, the skin feels better."

"Can I touch it?" Tika asked.

"I'm not sure. It got hard when Ram...Liam touched it."

Moira and Tika stood and stared, neither saying a word.

They all looked to the door when it opened and Ramirez entered. "Can she walk around?"

Moira seemed startled by the question. "I suppose." Kaalinda thought that Ramirez had been a bit brusque.

"Then let her get dressed." He tossed some clothes on the foot of the bed. Kaalinda recognized her pants but not the shirt. "I've got permission to show her the ponds before we take her back to the base."

Moira watched her son.

Ramirez kept his face averted. He left quickly, closing the door behind him more forceful than necessary.

Kaalinda struggled with the blankets, trying to swing her feet over the side so she could stand. The bandages on her back pulled, and she could feel the seam of the cut stretch, but it didn't hurt. "I'm fine. Help me get dressed, please? I really want to see the ponds."

Tika walked around the bed and shook out theshirt. After a moment, Moira grasped Kaalinda's arm and helped her stand. Her legs were shaky, but she stayed upright. By the time she was fully dressed, the shaky feeling in her legs had passed, and Kaalinda was sure she'd be able to walk around without incident.

Moira shook her head, but opened the door. She started back, surprised by what she found there.

"Is she ready?"

Ramirez had been waiting.

"Yes, but don't let her overdo it. She's still weak."

"Fine." Ramirez poked his head in the room. His eyes found Kaalinda's. "Let's go. We're wasting time we don't have."

Kaalinda walked to the door. "I take it we're leaving soon?"

"Yeah."

They were silent walking down the corridor. Most everyone they met wore the same drab green uniforms, some with white lab coats over, others with jackets or sweaters of a different color. Ramirez explained that the jacket or sweater color told you what part of the base they worked on, or their job.

The base was large—larger than Kaalinda had expected.

"How large is the base?"

"Large." Ramirez wouldn't say any more than that.

Kaalinda could smell the plants when they got close to the gardens. She could feel the moisture in the air. She took a deep breath in, letting the odors fill her.

She gasped when they finally reached the ponds.

They seemed to go on forever. Room after room, pond after pond with green algae floating on the surface of the water. Large windows let them see into the rooms.

"Why the windows?"

"It lets us see who is inside without having to open a door and let the humidity and heat out. It took us a while to figure it out, but we lost crops and had a lot of trouble keeping the ones going that survived until we realized that every time we opened a door to enter, we changed the environment in the rooms."

They were stopped outside a room that appeared to have a living green carpet it was so thick on the water. A worker was inside, examining the plants, picking samples from the water, then putting them back in.

"So, it's just plant material?"

"Yeah. There's some process I don't understand that they use to turn it into the fabric for the suits. But basically, it's just plants." Ramirez looked at her.

"When we were on base, and you were in your suit, did it ever talk to you?"

Ramirez laughed. "Talk to me?" He shook his head. "No, it never talked to me."

"Mine did. It still does." She could hear the faint chatter of the fabric now, listened to it tell her about her pulse rate (it was a bit high), the amount of iron in her blood (it was down), and that she would be starting her menstrual cycle in the next week. That was different. She hadn't had one of those since she'd been sterilized.

Oh, right—it had been reversed.

"It also reversed my sterilization." Why the fuck had she said that out loud?

Ramirez looked at her, leaning against the window of the pond room. "How?"

Kaalinda shrugged. "I don't know. Dr. Simons told me it had been reversed by the suit when I was at the research hospital."

"Red, all I got from my suit was a stat display in front of my left eye when I asked for it."

Kaalinda nodded. She had known her suit was different. And Ramirez and Captain Carson had said something about her getting one of the earlier models because it was dark. And Bromley had said as much at the laboratory: Kaalinda had gotten an original.

The door opened and the worker came out, a small sample of the lush green plant in a vial. The fabric on Kaalinda's shoulder pulsed and shuddered. Kaalinda raised her right hand to her left shoulder, rubbing at the fabric that clung to her skin beneath her shirt.

"What's wrong?" Ramirez had straightened from the window and reached out for her arm, remembering at the last second not to touch her.

"The fabric reacted to the plants, I guess. Or the heat and humidity that came out of the room when the door opened."

"Are you okay?"

"I'm fine." But she still rubbed her shoulder.

Hungry. The word whispered in the back of her mind. *Food.* "I think it needs nourishment. Do you think it could eat the plants?"

No. Sunlight.

"Can I go into one of the rooms?"

Ramirez frowned and sighed. "I can ask. Don't go dripping plants all over your shoulder, though. I'm not sure what my dad would do."

"Okay." Kaalinda looked into the pond room in front of them. Light shone brightly into the room, fed by reflective tunnels that went to the surface.

"Wait here." Ramirez walked down the corridor and opened a door half-way down. He poked his head into the room and spoke to someone inside. He backed up and someone came out. It was woman wearing a dark green lab coat over the drab green uniform.

"Liam says you want to go into one of the rooms."

"Yes. I would like to, if that's okay."

The woman frowned. "We don't usually allow visitors into the rooms."

Kaalinda nodded. "I understand." She was disappointed, but this was a military base and she was considered the enemy. Or at least, not an ally.

Something beeped on Ramirez. He picked up a slim black device and held it to his ear, listening to whoever had called him.

"Okay. We'll be right there." He pressed a button on the unit and put it back in the side pocket on his jacket. "It doesn't matter. We've run out of time. We have to go. They're taking you back to base now."

Kaalinda nodded. She looked longingly into the pond room, then turned to leave.

Ramirez led the way, and Kaalinda had to jog a bit to keep up with his long strides.

"Hey, slow down. I can't keep up." The jogging was making her back hurt.

Ramirez immediately stopped. "Sorry. I forgot you were hurt."

They walked the rest of the way. Kaalinda found herself dragging her feet, trying to delay the inevitable departure. She didn't want to leave.

When they reached the others, Ian was pacing. "What took you so long?"

"I had trouble keeping up." Kaalinda spoke before Ramirez could start an argument with his father. "I didn't expect to get so tired so suddenly. I'm sorry."

Ian glared at her but said nothing.

Tika was standing beside Moira, practically jumping in excitement. Kaalinda had to smile at the girl's joy. "Happy to be going home, eh?"

The girl nodded. "I can't wait to see my dad. And then my mom. I bet they'll be really happy that I'm okay and not dead."

"I bet they will. They'll probably spoil you rotten for a while."

Tika giggled. "I know. I can't wait."

They followed Ian to a waiting transport. It was painted in green and brown camouflage, and the back dropped down to make a ramp so they could walk into the back. The seats were solid benches that ran down each side, rather than the plush individual seats that Kaalinda was familiar with. She thought this design might be a tad more functional for moving troops.

She and Tika sat on one side. Ian and Ramirez sat on the other.

"Sir. Shouldn't you stay here, at base?" A Major addressed Ramirez's father.

"No. I'm go to see them safely to the drop-off point."

Three additional soldiers loaded into the transport carrying sidearms. The driver started the engine and the back hatch pulled up and closed.

They left, the pitch of the engine's whine getting higher.

The windows to the outside were small, but Tika rose onto her knees and watched the changing landscape. It moved by fast, the trees a blur of sickly green, brown, and yellow.

"We're going to drop you about a mile and a half from the base. There's another transport due to go by in about fifteen minutes. You should be able to walk to the base without problem if you miss it, or it isn't traveling on schedule. We'd get you closer, but we don't dare."

Kaalinda nodded, shifting on her seat.

Ramirez sat across from her, staring at a spot above her head. He looked upset, his jaw clenched and his nostrils flared.

She was anxious, and if she was honest, she wasn't sure why. Was she upset? Yes. She wanted to stay here—with Ramirez.

She looked at him, really looked at him. She could see his pulse beat at his throat. Knew that the clenched jaw meant he was angry. That the flared nostrils meant he was anxious and trying to breathe to calm himself down.

The transport slowed.

"We'll be walking for a bit. Their sensors could pick up the transport if we get too much closer." Ian rose from his seat and walked to the back of the transport. The back lowered. Ian stepped on it and jumped to the ground before it was all the way down.

The armed soldiers sighed and rolled their eyes and followed him.

"Doesn't like to wait, does he?" Kaalinda asked the question while restraining Tika.

"Nope." Ramirez's answer was terse. "Let's go."

Tika ran out the back and joined the soldiers and Ian.

Kaalinda took her time. Her back was beginning to ache. And she felt like crying.

What was the matter with her?

Maybe it was her impending cycle. She hadn't had one in a while.

The group walked through the woods; one armed soldier performed reconnaissance, scoping the lay of the land in advance of the main group; one walked in front with Ian, his weapon out and ready; and one walked behind them, also with his weapon drawn and ready to fire. They were all alert, walking slow, with purpose, muscles tense and ready.

The forest was dense. Kaalinda hadn't expected it to be dense. She had heard so much about the poor state of the environment. She could even hear the scurrying sounds of animals in the brush.

A few dozen feet from the edge of the forest, the recon soldier waited in a crouch, watching the road that could be seen in the opening beyond. They all stopped and squatted, waiting, listening.

They heard nothing.

Ian turned to Kaalinda and Tika. "The base is to the right. Keep to the road. The transport will be by shortly and they should find you. If not, keep walking and you will run right into the main gate."

Ian glanced at Ramirez before redirecting his gaze back to Kaalina. "I trust that neither of you will mention where you really were. You'll tell them you have spent the last four days in the woods, lost. You went in to get out of the heat, and wandered too far in."

"What about my back?"

"If anyone has to look at you, request Dr. Simons. He won't ask too many questions."

So, Kaalinda thought, *Dr. Simons*. It didn't surprise her, not really.

She looked at the road. Heat waves rolled up from the dark, hard surface, making the trees on the other side wavy.

Her parents would have been told she was dead, killed in the transport explosion. For her to come back, would make them happy. But what would it really change?

They had lost Pol, their first born, and that had caused irrevocable damage to their family. Her return wouldn't reverse it, and of it. She couldn't bring back the farm, that had been destroyed.

What was there for her to go back to?

Kaalinda glanced to the side, her gaze sliding over the hard expression on Ramirez' face.

Tika wound her arms around her neck and kissed her on the cheek. "Bye, Kaalinda." She whispered the words into her ear. "I'll be okay. I can make it to the base."

"Tika..."

How did the girl know?

Smiling, Tika leaned back, tilting her head toward Ramirez. "Don't worry about me. I've been on my own on those transports lots of times, travelling, so I'm not scared."

Ian frowned and so did Ramirez. The other three soldiers were looking around, paying no attention to their conversation, concerned instead with their surroundings and the possibility of enemy soldiers finding them.

Tika walked out of the forest to the road. The girl looked to her left and right, then began walking to the right, staying to the side of the road. She didn't wave. She didn't look back.

Kaalinda stayed crouched in the forest, watching.

"Red…"

She didn't turn her head. "I can't go back there. There's nothing for me there anymore. Going back won't change anything, won't help anything."

"MacReady. What are you talking about?" Ian's voice was harsh.

"I want to stay with you. Stay at the base."

"Damn it." Ian spat on the ground.

"I'm a farmer." She shrugged. "I think I could help here.

"You want to stay?" Ramirez asked the question.

Kaalinda turned to look at him. "Yes, Liam. I want to stay."

Liam grabbed her right hand and tugged her along. "Let's get back then, before we're caught." They could hear the dull whine of the electric transport coming down the road. "The transport is coming and will find Tika. She'll be fine."

The moved farther back into the forest. They could hear the squeal of the transport's brakes and the shouting when those onboard saw the girl.

Ian nodded to the soldiers and they moved through the trees, keeping quiet all the way back to the transport. It was waiting where they had left it, the driver standing guard outside, his weapon at the ready.

He only raised his eyebrows when he saw Kaalinda.

Liam ignored him and hauled Kaalinda into the back of the transport, never once letting go of her hand

www.ingramcontent.com/pod-product-compliance
Lightning Source LLC
Chambersburg PA
CBHW060440310726
48977CB00001B/272